I0589135

Yearning

Marlene Archie

Published and Distributed By
MeiraMa Production
P.O. Box 722
Spring House, Pennsylvania 19477

Cover and Interior Design by:
TWA Solutions
www.twasolutions.com

ISBN: 978-0-692-52399-5

First print: October 2015

For inquires, contact the publisher.

ACKNOWLEDGMENTS

For the notion of *Yearning*, I must thank my earthly father, Jesse, who came from my grandmother, Catherine, who came from Nana Mert and so on and so on.

Thanks be to God, my heavenly father, for the labor, and for granting me the critical thought this book required. Thank you Jesus, for providing what I needed, particularly the resolve to revisit, revise, and reorder my stories.

Thank you to all my readers, including my family for your endurance—for staying the course with me on this emotional journey.

Thanks to Victoria Christopher Murray and Associates, for lessons well learned.

This is for Catherine.

CONTENTS

Just Us

DURING HIS FINAL WEEKS of tenth grade, my brother, Shams, got ambushed by a group of boys outside school. Afterward, he changed, except we didn't talk about it. He dodged chores, and devoted more of his time to reading. He used the sympathy he received for his mishap as an opportunity. So long as he could read, he invested minimal time and attention to the equal duties we had previously shared doing household tasks.

That summer, after the incident and right before he turned sixteen, Shams had cajoled Mother into agreeing he should stop doing kitchen chores. He had performed below standards while on kitchen detail and was constantly sent back to do it over. Shams kept doing the kitchen over and over. He wouldn't do it right and Mother grew tired of his behavior. So she excused him from kitchen duties permanently, and that job was left eternally to my sister, Lorraine, and me.

"That's not fair," Lorraine and I said. But Mother had made up her mind. She said something about our brother having tougher chores, like taking out the garbage and yard work, in keeping with his African American male peers in the neighborhood. Didn't want him to appear soft in our public housing court, where hardness was a part of our daily survival.

Moving into 'public housing,' as she had called it, required that we 'develop thick skin,' my mother had said. Because we were Black, and also without consistent support from my father, we had to protect ourselves with a fighting spirit. After the incident, the calmness she showed must have been due to some kind of divine intervention 'cause I didn't want to believe she no longer had the will of a rebel.

When I first knew it, in 1961, James W. Johnson projects in North Philadelphia, was filled with thug activity. We often witnessed and had to navigate around open drug dealing, idle youth, and gang war. That was part of why it was hard for me to understand why my mother let my scheming brother off from kitchen duty permanently. Especially since Shams teased me and Lorraine all the time about having to do chores he didn't have to do. And even though he boasted of having convinced Mother it was sissified for a male child to do dishes, I believed it had more to do with the events that took place during his sophomore school year. I was also struck by the sudden resolve that came over my mother, and how she appeared slow to anger.

She had always said, "Don't be a tattle tale. Do what you can; can what you do." I think it meant keep some things to yourself, choose battles wisely, and own what you do. She also said, "Pray much for the good deeds of others, and pray also for evildoers because God looks high and He looks low." I did not know then that her words would be elevated through the real meaning of what she was saying.

She constantly reminded me that it didn't pay to fret about the uncertainties of the low life reality that was our home. Only the Lord could keep a child safe from the mishaps that plagued Johnson Housing. But the nasty way outsiders treated 'project' folks was part of what made me depend on and love the people who resided there, even with my fears about how secure we really were. While God's Word also said that worrying would not add anything good, I still did. And I had a nerve-wracking feeling about my siblings that dreadful afternoon nonetheless.

The rain hit the roof and ran down the cloudy window. As I looked down, it flowed out the end of the down-spout stapled to the brick wall between Ms. Fannie's house and ours. They were late; and with the rain and all, it felt like something must have happened. My stomach was churning sort of like the feeling when I had to stand in school and recite something.

Without a call from their school by now to report their bus as late, the churning continued. *Should I call Momma at work? Or just do my homework?* These questions marched into my mind. Humming to myself, I sat down at the oval kitchen table with the low hanging light, pencil between my front teeth and began to review the day's lesson.

Earlier, my focus was on the happenings at my own school. Many of the mostly African American teachers at Pratt Elementary talked about Negro affairs. Pratt sat just beyond the last row of low rise houses in Johnson Homes and was where most of the young people from the projects were enrolled. Some of the older kids were bused out of the community, and still a few went to the other neighborhood elementary, William Dick. Most of us just called it Dick for short.

Animated, my teachers would wave their arms and move around the room, stopping next to this one or that one, trying to keep our attention. *Why they do that?* I wondered. *After class, I'm gon' ask.*

"Ms. Jenkins, why you always talking about Negroes?"

"Why, Anel, like all of you, I am also Black."

"Well, how come your hair straight and your skin white?"

"We come in all colors, and my hair does not revert because I perm it regularly. Now go on home and do your lesson."

On the walk home, my thoughts drifted to my sister and brother. They would be home shortly after me; we were gon' eat snacks and watch Soul Train. They be dancing like nobody's business on that show; it just made me wanna dance, too. We might listen to some Wild Man Steve comedy. He's so funny, we crack up. Especially since we not supposed to listen to him anyway. Momma won't know what we been up to if we put the records back right. Big brother always said, "Momma is on a need-to-know basis." Shams was clever, but now that I'd arrived home and my brother and sister weren't there, I wondered, how come they so late?

In the '60s, being bused out to the white neighborhood was something like a good opportunity. Although, it was what Mother decided that I, the youngest of three, wouldn't do. I would go to Pratt Elementary while Lorraine and Shams were bused to Jones High School in the greater Northeast. That section of Philadelphia was mostly white. The schools were said to be better, and their buildings were fancier than the ones in the Black neighborhoods. It was like some of us even believed their lemonade was colder. And some parents who chose busing were said to be sort of radical.

My mother was no nonsense. If what you told her didn't add up, then it made no sense. And if it made no sense, then she didn't want to hear it. As a bank officer, she had to settle big accounts all day long. At the end of the day, all figures had to add up. If her totals were even a few cents off, she would do a recount until she got it right. That's the way she was about most things at home, too. If you didn't do it right, do it over, period.

My siblings had no input into the decision for them to attend Jones. That was left to Mother, who rarely consulted with Dad on such matters. Dad must have had his mind on other pressing matters since he was usually "away," as mother put it.

My thoughts returned to the present. Generally, they came in right after me 'cause Mother always told them to get on the first bus. That was the 2:55. *They should have been here by now.*

Just as I was about to pick up the receiver, I heard familiar footsteps. Seemed like they were moving kinda slow rather than hurrying out the rain; then again it sounded like only one instead of two. Lorraine's sad eyes greeted me sitting on the stool by the phone.

My sister was petite. She was four foot ten inches tall and weighed less than one hundred pounds. She had jet black hair worn usually with bangs, and she was a medium brown complexion. Lorraine was four years my senior, and at fourteen, she was already showing signs of a budding chest and a round behind.

"You ain't call Momma, did you?" Lorraine asked me.

"No. What happened?"

Her bangs were matted against her forehead under her rain-soaked scarf. Black smudges that must have been from the mascara she would sometimes sneak on her eyelashes after leaving home for school, were between her checks and eyes. With sagging shoulders, she pursed her lips, shook her head and said, "Momma always told him to get on the first bus, but he didn't listen. We gon' have to go over to Dr. Clark's and see about him. They had to take him over there since some of them white boys caught him wandering over by the pretzel stand and they chased him."

"And?"

"They threw him on the ground. From the bus window I was praying the bus attendant, Ms. Wiley, would see what was happening. I was so scared. They took something out of their pockets, one of them boys, and poured it on him. I put my hands up to my face when I saw the flame. He was twisting and turning trying to get up and flap out the fire. That's when the attendant turned and noticed what was happening. It was lighter fluid."

"Oh, Lord." My stomach was in an uproar. "How'd they get him to Dr. Clark? Is he gon' be okay? Rain, don't we have to call Mother now?" I had so many questions that I kept rambling on, while Lorraine looked down at her feet, puffed out her cheeks and exhaled. Then she looked at me.

"We not gon' call Momma now. We gon' go over there and see what Dr. Clark says." She turned off the light switch and turned toward the door. I followed and prayed everything would be alright. We hurried into the rain that came softly now. We walked down 24th Street toward Diamond. I looked over at Lorraine.

"What we gon' tell Mother when she comes home?"

"I don't know. I wish Shams had listened, but I'm glad Ms. Wiley was there." Lorraine's voice came out in puffs like when a person speaks while running fast. "After Ms. Wiley saw what was happening, with her bowlegged self, she jetted off that bus. She put something on Brother's chest, while he was on the ground. Then she said, 'Move back,' to the people watching. I didn't know what to do; I called his name and then went after Ms. Wiley. I hesitated because I didn't want to look at what the fire had done to him. He was sitting up by the time I reached him, and then my eyes began to water.

"He looked up at me and Ms. Wiley. She had her arm around his shoulder. He said, 'I'm okay; it don't hurt too bad.' He bent his chin toward his chest that looked darker than usual. Ms. Wiley helped him to his feet and together we walked him inside the building."

Lorraine and I had rounded the corner onto Diamond, and we had a little more than three blocks to go.

Lorraine continued. "When I got back on the bus, Sylvia asked, 'Where did they take your brother?' You know her, Brandon's sister. We usually sit together on the bus. The other students strained their necks to hear our conversation. I shrugged my shoulders and said, 'They took him to the nurse. I hope she's still there. Sometimes she leaves early.'

"She asked, 'Is he hurt bad? What did those boys do to him?' I told her what I saw them do. Then she asked, 'Are you serious?' Then she said, 'The kids that are bused here don't get no respect. I hope something is done about this, but I doubt it. After all, we just Negroes, and they are white.'

"We waited about forty-five minutes before Ms. Wiley brought Shams on the bus. He looked exhausted. His eyes were red and, as he moved into the first seat up front, he just held his hand up against the side of his head. Ms. Wiley climbed up behind him and faced us. Some had eyes big as saucers; others' mouths were frozen in O shapes, while I just stared straight ahead; I couldn't move.

"Ms. Wiley said something about it being unfortunate that some students chose to express dissent with violence; she said that Shams would be okay once he got treated for his injuries by a doctor. I don't remember her mentioning the fire she had put out on his chest. Eventually, I had crept up to the seat behind Brother and whispered through the cracks. 'You okay for real?' He gave a slight nod, but his eyes were closed, his head back. Ms. Wiley sat down beside him and the driver took off in a hurry.

"At Dr. Clark's, only Ms. Wiley and Shams got off; the bus driver took the rest of us to our stop. Then I hurried to get you. I knew you would think something was wrong 'cause you always had the 'shine.' You could always sense when things went wrong."

She looked over at me with pleading eyes, as if wanting to get this over with. We had reached the doctor's office.

Dr. Clark stood by the cot that Brother laid on when the nurse, Ms. Marge, ushered us into the room. Addressing the both of us, the doctor said, "He will be okay. I dressed his burns and gave him something for the pain. He might want to lie down for a while, but we are going to keep the burn covered for a week and then put salve on it; Ms. Marge will see that you get some. His normal color there on his chest will return in a couple of weeks. It could have been worse."

The doctor shot a serious look at Lorraine. Then Shams slowly sat up and began to put on his shirt. Lorraine and I rushed over to help him.

Dr. Clark looked down at the chart in his hand; he wrote something there. "What did your mother say?" He was looking from Lorraine to Shams, to me. I spoke up.

"She don't know. We haven't told her. She still at work."

Dr. Clark, a grey-haired stoic man, knew our family well. He knew Mother worked every day and single-handedly took care of us. He tended to most of our medical needs, even at times when we couldn't pay. He did that for some of the families in our court; he had a good reputation for helping Black folks. I shifted my weight to one foot and the doctor seemed to read my eagerness. I just wanted to tell Mother and get my brother home.

"You can take him home and let him lie down. I will make a call to the school so that those boys who did this will be dealt with. Not to worry, now go on home."

Dr. Clark was light skinned, and had freckles on his face. He was tall and his eyes were soft. He conveyed strength, wisdom, and gentleness all at the same time. He guided Brother off the table and handed something to Lorraine. Then he bent down to face me. "Young lady, listen to your sister. Everything will be okay." His narrowed eyes and pressed lips suggested compassion for our circumstances. We all turned to go.

Lorraine asked our brother, "Are you really okay?"

"I will be. We don't have to tell Mom. She has enough. Dr. Clark will take care of it. He told me so. I told him who did this. Let's go home."

"How's he gon' take care of it?" I asked.

Brother took my hand in his and squeezed. He looked down at me and said, "The best way he can. Now don't you go telling. I'm gon' be alright."

"You sure?"

"I'm sure." He smiled.

I learned later Dr. Clark had a sister who worked as an administrator in the Northeast School District. She called the principal of Jones High School. Whatever she said must have resulted in more than what Mother may have been able to get done on her own. According to Brother, the boys responsible for his burns were expelled and a special assembly was held on bullying where Shams was called on to speak. He also said that it was awkward for him to share some things with Mother, and what had happened was one of them.

He said that it was more bearable to confront the boys who set fire to him with Dr. Clark's, rather than Mother's involvement, and what was more important was that some things be handled between men. I had not thought of Brother as a man until then; to me he'd been just Brother. But thereafter, he seemed more grown-up.

Perhaps it was due to the book he read, *The Autobiography of Malcolm X*, that had been recommended by Dr. Clark. Shams had finally told me the doctor suggested that book on a note he gave to Lorraine when we were in his office. That kind of reading could be good for him, I thought. Two things made me think that: Ms. Jenkins said, 'reading autobiography gave readers a basis for examining their own lives;' and the doctor said it was 'well written;' what the doctor actually said, Shams told me, was the book 'powerfully hid and revealed X's hatred,' and 'all young people should read it.' *Could it possibly be the book that changed him?* I thought.

After some months had passed, I could not hold it any longer and I told Mother some of what had happened. We were plucking green beans at the kitchen table.

Mother said, "I found out recently what had happened from Ms. Marge. It was upsetting, but I don't know how that was kept from me for as long as it was."

"I wanted to tell you, but Rain and Shams said not to. Then Dr. Clark said that I should listen to my sister. I did, because I thought she didn't want you to have to fight with those white folks at Jones. She said white people don't really want us there anyway, and would never have made the punishment fit the crime for those boys no matter how wrong they were."

"Well, I did get some relief knowing that my girls took care of things, that those perpetrators were expelled with the help of Dr. Clark, and that the burns were not more severe."

The corners of my mouth turned up. It felt like things had turned out as they should. Normally, Mother would have upset somebody's world for messing with her children. She would have told somebody off. And she just may have beaten the devil out of us for keeping what we did from her. Instead, she stared straight ahead, and with a quickness, her fingers kept moving.

She said, "You have to ask, what kind of person does that to another? We must pray without ceasing not just for us, but for those boys, too."

"But those boys are haters." *They* may be hurting yes, but they hurt others, like Shams, more.

"Those boys didn't just injure Shams, they've injured themselves also. In more ways than they know."

"They was probably already injured. I mean they were hurt in some way; what or whoever taught them hate, hurt them. And hurt people, hurt others. That may be their kind of justice."

"Their kind of anything hasn't worked for us. We could have gained a lot from correct punishment, but that'll never happen since we ain't ever been equal."

"How come?"

"White people do not want equality, so we have to fight for it. We have to be smart about it and sometimes more aggressive.

"I think that X man said something like that, 'By any means necessary.'"

"Yes," she said. "He may be about violence, but some of what he believed seemed to be right on point. One thing is for sure, he described our situation correctly when he suggested, 'Instead of it being jail for them, it's been jail and injustice for us.'"

Chotah

You must live within your sacred truth.
– Hausa proverb

August 1990 – 30th Street Station – Philadelphia, Pennsylvania

AS I BOARDED THE huge Amtrak Acela, carrying a sack of snacks, books, electronic games, and blankets for the boys, I ushered them on ahead of me. Twelve-year-old Raoul was thin and lanky, wearing braces as he guided his little brother, Semaj, toward the rear of the car. The trip was organized by Ditmar, a social worker like me who was finally able to treat her two girls, Kara, twelve, and Whitney, ten, to their dream trip to Disney World in Florida. Ditmar had said it might be good for me to just take the boys and my mind on a hiatus and I had agreed.

I saw her halfway in, toward the back of the train already seemingly settled in. She waved and I waved back while getting the boys situated in their section a few seats up from where I would sit with my friend.

"Hi, Kara. Hi, Whitney," I said to Ditmar's girls as Raoul looked around for a place to set his bag of comic books.

19

"Wazup?" he asked them.

"Hi," they said back in unison as he pointed to where five-year-old Semaj would sit. I handed his brother his Donkey Kong game, as I said, "You guys gon' be okay here?"

They both nodded, looking down at their things rather than at the girls' wide smiles.

I smiled back and said, "Y'all ready for Disney?"

"Oh yeah," said Kara.

Whitney said, "Can't wait."

My eyes scanned the rest of the car as I moved sideways for another passenger to pass in the aisle, and proceeded with my bags toward Ditmar.

"Hey, girl. How you doing?" she asked as I approached.

"I'm doing," I responded as I glided into the seat beside her. I placed my bags in the area in front of my feet, removed one of the books I carried, and exhaled. Then I turned toward Ditmar and said, "How are you?"

Ditmar was a tall thin woman who took charge at work. A kind woman. Today, she had coiffed her light brown hair up in a loose bun and wore tennis shoes and jeans. She had a throaty voice, grayish eyes and smooth milk chocolate skin. Most times we referred to each other by last names since at work, our daily assignments were usually arranged on a chart for intake workers that way.

She smiled at me and asked, "What's up with you, Sourcream?"

"Other than thinking too hard about how I am going to get through all of this, I am fine." My reference was to my recent divorce and being a single parent in a city where we rarely witnessed acts of kindness. This concerned me in terms of the negative images the boys observed, not to mention that being on leave from work was a bit concerning, too. Anyway, I thought, I needed this break from work to help me sort things through. I would figure things out, I was sure, and my thoughts drifted to Kevin.

I had divorced this man, yet I still thought of him regularly. Too regular to be healthy, but I couldn't help it. I turned toward Ditmar.

"This much loss ain't natural."

"What do you mean?"

"I mean, losing a husband to divorce, and most of my close girlfriends to death; that's not natural."

"You mean your girls from the projects?"

I was not surprised that Ditmar knew what losses I was talking about since I talked so much about this to her, seeing death up close and going through a divorce so young.

"Yeah, Nae, Karen, and Quenchetta; and now Kevin." At work, Ditmar and I were close associates. I confided in her about other things, too, like childcare issues, from choosing affordable day care in close proximity to our work site, to relying on family members to fill in the gaps when the childcare costs became challenging. A decade older, she had experienced some of the same issues I faced, and we were assigned to the same unit at work. So, our friendship had evolved; she had always encouraged me and said that I would be fine. I liked hearing that although

I was often doubtful, especially when I started suspecting drug use by my husband. I had trouble concentrating at times, and Ditmar willingly covered for me when I would get behind on my assigned tasks. She was a special co-worker to have. A blessing.

"You thought about talking to a professional about your feelings? You know we have the Employees Assistance Program."

"Yes, but you need to hang out your own shingle, girl, because I don't get the same relief with a stranger that I get from talking to you." At this, she laughed; a low chuckle. I often did most of the talking, and she did the listening; we frequently characterized our talks as therapeutic.

"It's good to talk it out, and we have more than twenty hours to do that and pass the time. Why do you think your divorce is a loss? Do you really associate it with not having your girls anymore? That's different. You have a lot of living to do; you're barely thirty-five. I think divorce is just making your feelings about your younger years more profound. You'll move through this. You have to for them."

Her gaze was on our children who were chatting and looking around at all the hustle and bustle going on in the train. Several families were talking with their children. Some were rifling through bags. Others moved toward the dining car where they could purchase, sit, and eat their snacks away from where they seemingly would ride for an entire day.

An attendant in a conductor's uniform belted out, "Tickets," drowning out the multitude of voices as the train hissed and lurched forward. And Ditmar and I settled in for my story of loss. As she lay back against the headrest, I hoped to release what was heavy on my mind.

I recounted losing my best friends, my Chotahs, in the prime of our lives. And as the train roared toward Florida, I relived that evening after work when I went to the hospital to see Nae unbeknownst for the last time. Indeed, the shock of losing Karen was also still with me.

August 1987 – Philadelphia, Pennsylvania

It was early evening and the deluge of folks that usually came during the final fraction of visiting hours hadn't yet arrived, so I pulled into the parking lot of the Philadelphia Germantown Medical Center off Wister Street and spotted a parking space rather easily. I paced my large frame up the hill toward the hospital and entered the double doors. Although I was dragging, I still had to go see Nae. She had been admitted earlier, calling me at work to say she was making her usual trip to the hospital after one of her frequent 'coughing spells' became uncontrollable and had rendered her so weak, she could barely stand. After obtaining a visitor's pass, I made my way over to the elevator and wondered how she was doing. Growing up together in Raymond Rosen Housing, we had relied on each other as youngsters; we still did so, even more since we had become mothers.

Entering her room, I found Nae sitting up in the bed. Grinning sheepishly, she said, "Hey, girl. I knew you would come." She said this between violent coughs. With her head tilted back on the pillow, covers drawn up chest high, and eyelids drooped, she used several tissues to collect the phlegm coming up between hacking spells.

A nurse entered the room and headed straight toward the monitor beside Nae's bed. Without acknowledging either one of us, she immediately began examining the blinking lights and the contents of a little container attached to a tube above Nae's head. The container, a clear plastic cylinder thingy, contained what looked like mucous tainted with blood. I looked away from the container, focusing on Nae. "How you doing?"

"I'm okay." Coughing sounds filled the room. "Just tired of all this coughing, it's making my chest hurt bad."

"What are they saying?"

"They not telling me nothing; just keep watching that thing up there and looking at me wide-eyed." Between her coughing, Nae nods toward the nurse who was focused on the container thingy that had a tube attached and through which a mucous mixture was rising; there was a catheter in Nae's nose that must have extended down her esophagus, the other end of which was connected to the container. With all of this going on and between coughs, Nae asked, "Did you call and check on your guys?"

"They're okay. I let them know I would be stopping to see you. Kevin ain't got nothing else to do, but feed the boys and clean the kitchen anyway. He is still pretending that he cannot go into work. But it's a good thing he's always sensitive to your illness, so I won't stay long. What about Lil Anthony?"

"I told him to go over to Ms. LuBelle's if I was not home by now. She already called and said he was watching television. Chotah, do me a favor."

"What?"

"If anything happens, take Lil Anthony to his father. I don't want my sisters with him because they messing with that stuff and can't get their lives together. You know what crack can do; look at some of the folks we grew up with. They turning into nightwalkers—sleeping during the day, out searching for a hit at night. That's just one image that scares me.

"And then every time I look at the nurse, her eyes get so wide. I don't know what she looking scared for, I'm the one in the hospital bed. What do you think all this stuff is?" Nae was referring to the increasing mucous matter she was collecting in the tissues in her hand, never mind the matter that was pushing its way up the tubing.

"Nothing is going to happen. I'm not sure what that stuff is, but it has a little blood in it. That must mean your chest is inflamed, so you had better take it easy and stop talking. You really are coughing up a storm. Stop worrying about stuff. You ain't going nowhere tonight. I'll talk to you tomorrow."

"Yeah, I'd better just lie still; the nurse looks as if she seen a ghost." Sounds of coughing continued. "You'd better get going. I am just going to rest up. Call me tomorrow. You goin' to work tomorrow?"

I kissed her cheek, preparing to leave, and swung my bag up on my shoulder.

"Yeah, Chotah, I'll call you and I will pray that you get some rest. Talk to ya later." I made my way over to the door and forced a smile, glanced back at Nae, and then headed back down the hall leading to the elevators and the exit that would take me to the hilly path winding down toward the parking lot.

Heading home down the other end of Wister Street toward Stenton Avenue, my mind was on the rest of the evening's tasks: taking care of the guys, reading a little, and getting ready for the next day. My thoughts moved to Kevin who hadn't been going into work. Therefore, he would have taken care of household chores like cleaning the kitchen and getting the boys ready for bed. Kevin had his good points. He certainly was good at domestic chores, but something was going on with him that I couldn't quite put my finger on. Especially since he wasn't going to work on the regular. I was becoming increasingly bothered by things that had a lot to do with Kevin's behavior and, at times, the intense gaze on Raoul's face.

Raoul had left a note for me on the dining room table that next morning. It was distressing. He talked about how worried he was about Dad. Said that his father seemed tensed, and was drawin', which meant something like short tempered. He said that Dad's nose was always running, he was always sniffling and sweating a lot, and he was often hoarse like he had a cold. Said, when they went to the market together, he had to help his father more than the usual; said Dad seemed weak.

That boy was always writing. He was able to put his expressions to paper when he was about seven. Been doing that ever since. But that note made me sad. Made me think about my mother. Also I was thinking about getting into work and then visiting with Nae after. A lot was on my mind, not to mention Kevin.

Mama had warned me about Kevin, but did I listen? No, and because we were married for five years and together for more than fifteen, I thought I had proved Mama wrong about Kevin. Mama had always been there for me, but I really didn't need her in all of my business, especially when it came to Kevin, even though, when it came down to it, she was usually right on point.

Truly a miracle, Mama was able to raise three children on her own after her husband, my father, veered off to the left and served more than twenty-five years in the penitentiary. Before the penitentiary, right out of high school, in a row, my parents had a baby girl, a boy, and then me.

She raised us in the 1960s in Raymond Rosen. Like other parents in the turbulent '60s, when Mayor Rizzo thought nothing of beating Black folks over the head to solve the gang war problems, and while Martin Luther King, Jr. encouraged folks to march for freedom. The Black Panthers and the Black Muslims were regulars in the community. Muslims sold bean pies and *The Final Call* on street corners, and served breakfast to the needy children who would otherwise go to school hungry; and while James Brown was singng "I'm Black and I'm Proud," Mama taught us to stay in school and maintain a sense of dignity, determination, and mutual devotion to our friends and to one another.

In the early years, the summer of 1964, at eight years old, NaeNae, Karen, Quenchetta and I took an oath to always look out for each other. Initially, it may have been Quenchetta who said we were Chotahs, making up a stylish name to flatter us. Over time, it became us. We went from being just girls to being extended family. And afterward, the mention of a classy young lady would be to call her a Chotah.

A year later, and three years after that, two awful, yet crucial events in American history unfolded. This we became vaguely aware of through hardened expressions. While crossing the Pettus Bridge to gain voting rights, Negroes were trampled, debased, and murdered in 1965 on what we now know as Bloody Sunday, and then in 1968 Martin Luther King, Jr. was assassinated. Those events most likely were a shadow of what was to come; the hushed discussions about them among the adults took on a somewhat vatic tone.

Black folks ceremoniously barred children from grown people's conversation, and the projects, contrary to how ominous life appeared, was once respectable housing; not that there wasn't the aggression, the sickness, drugs and violence that plagued the area now, but in another time and place, Raymond Rosen Housing held unforeseen promise for a few young people who would not likely have escaped a life designed to consume them—like the many other young people that life in the projects had claimed. It was not only poverty, which looked at first like the main culprit, but the gloom that seemed to engulf the area we had lived in that was a daily reminder of the grim chances of survival. Despite this, we learned to help and appreciate each other, values we got from grown folks. Although there was a complex web of troubles that went along with the overall sadism in public housing, some very good people came from Rosen from a time and place when the idea of aiding others ran deep into the spirit of a community.

And it was in those fecund years at Rosen that the principles of faith and self-determination were ingrained in the young people, especially the Chotahs.

Through the efforts of one community Mom and Reverend Sullivan's OIC program, in 1970, when we were fourteen NaeNae and I landed summer jobs. While we worked at the local library, Karen and her sisters created a singing group called the Brownetts, and Quenchetta took up sewing.

When we were seventeen, Christmastime 1973, NaeNae called to say she was moving in with her boyfriend. She said, "I'm getting a place with Tony in Germantown."

"Why do you have to move to Germantown to get a place?"

"That's where Tony wants to go, and if I'm going to make a break from the projects, it may as well be to Germantown with him."

Tony was a few years older than Nae. He appeared to be a responsible man because he worked and said he did not have children. So, the move did not seem like a totally bad idea at the time. I believed that, although physically apart, the Rosen Chotahs would remain spiritually connected. We had been so close, so early on that it was thought we could mentally connect when we put our minds to it. That was just part of being a Chotah.

NaeNae possessed an unassuming attitude, what one might call being a "little slow." She was average height, light skinned, had less body fat than me and more chores than most. One of five children, her father was a former cop dependent on alcohol and her mother was a nurse. On Saturday afternoons, we went roller skating in the school gymnasium at St. Elizabeth on Fountain Street. Often, we managed to get our chores done, and then we'd go to the Uptown Theatre on Broad Street. We'd see The Supremes and a couple of times we saw Jerry Butler.

Chotah Karen spent less of her time going to hear other singers and more coming up with her own songs to sing. Her family stayed in Rosen for some time after NaeNae and Tony hooked up and after my family had left. Of the four, Karen was the one in the group, who was very fair skinned. She had more body fat than Nae, and like me, she was thick. Karen was biracial, had long wavy hair, and a soothing temperament. She had a calming influence on the Chotahs. And she could sang. Her father was a very dark skinned African American married to her white mother, who was of German descent. She had two older sisters, both also fair skinned with wavy hair. Although Raymond Rosen was majority Black and Karen's parents were interracial, their difference did not affect the bond the Chotahs shared. We spent a lot of time in each other's homes including overnights. Another thing, another connection was that each one of us, except for Quenchetta, around the same time gave birth to sons.

Unlike Karen, Quenchetta was petite with keen features, and she was the smallest one in the group; smart and resourceful, Quenchetta, like me, excelled academically. She had four older siblings, three sisters and one brother. Her father, Mr. Cook, fixed watches on the weekends and her mother was a great cook, who also had beauty skills; that is, she could do a press and curl and she taught her daughters the trade. In addition to excelling in academics and doing hair, Quenchetta learned to sew.

Many of the young girls we grew up with learned to sew, but Quenchetta took it to another level. She created outfits that the Chotahs showed off on the weekends, which was another one of the things that had bonded us. That bond produced an unbroken circle in troubling times.

Three years before that crucial night when I visited Nae at the hospital, Quenchetta had called me on the phone. The bearer of wretched news that summer of 1984, she asked, "Maria, did you know Karen had sugar?"

"No. I didn't."

"After she had Benjy, it seems the doctors found she had diabetes. After she married Luke, she did not take her medicine regularly. Benjy was at school, and Luke was working. Her family found her unresponsive in her apartment. They rushed her to the hospital, but it was too late. Medically, she should have been on insulin; she had suffered a stroke and died."

Stunned, I had asked, "Died? When? She's twenty-nine. What about her son? He's about eight. I know because he was along with Raoul. How is he?" I asked so many questions, I was sure it was hard for Quenchetta to keep up.

When I took a breath, she answered, "He's fine, except his mother passed the other day; you know, you guys being so busy with parenting didn't really call me all that often. But my sister, Frieda, talked to Sylvia, who said arrangements were being made for her sister, and she said Benjy has his father. She added that when their parents divorced, their father, Mr. Brown, married a Black woman, and Mrs. Brown began living in a white world. Mrs. Brown remarried, too, to a white man and she no longer kept in contact with her daughters. Her spouse had a problem with African Americans, and perhaps it was easier or more convenient for Mrs. Brown to deny a part of herself for the sake of the marriage, especially since her daughters embraced their Black identity and all of them hooked up with African American men."

"I did know that Mrs. Brown had kind of removed herself from Karen's life, but Karen never mentioned her medical condition the last time we talked. We talked mainly about our future career plans and the boys. The music business, you know. And she always just said Benjy was growing and growing. This is terrible. What about the services?"

"They are working on this Saturday. Trying for the Church of the Advocate in North Philly."

"Have you spoken to NaeNae?"

"No. Chotah, but I know you will. I'll call you as soon as the family confirms."

After hearing from Sylvia, we had agreed to meet at the church. As I walked up, there was a long line of people gathered on the sidewalk waiting to go inside. After hugging Quenchetta and NaeNae, arm-in-arm we silently got in line. Approaching the casket as soft music played in the background, we heard another mourner say, "Something ain't right," to which we all nodded.

After viewing Karen in her green gown, looking as though she was asleep, the three of us took seats in the crowded church. But then we could clearly see what seemed wrong; rather than take seats in the pews, people began to file out of the church.

Were they going to come in with the family and then sit for the services, I wondered? I nudged Nae, and she nodded at Quenchetta, then we instinctively moved toward the front door.

Outside were throngs of people waiting around in front of the church where a long black limo with smoked windows appeared. After what seemed like an hour, Mrs. Brown, a thin, older white woman with limp brown hair emerged from the vehicle. She looked around at the sea of Black faces, many of which she did not seem to recognize, and made her way up the church steps as the people filed in behind her.

The service finally began with an opening prayer taken from Ecclesiastes 3:2. The Eulogist, a young medium brown skin man said, "There's an appointed time to die." Someone in the congregation cried out. The speaker said Karen gave her life to the Lord. He then spoke directly to Luke and Benjy saying, "Find comfort in family and in the Lord." A soloist gave a rendition of "Amazing Grace" that brought the people in attendance to tears. I grabbed Quenchetta and Nae's hands. We stood and hugged each other. Then everyone filed out of the church.

At the repast, Mr. Brown came over to where the three of us were eating. We each gave our condolences and he leaned in and gave each one of us a hug. Then he rejoined the other mourners including a young Black woman we later learned was his new wife. At the repast we also learned about Karen's mother's difficult decision to reveal her past at the risk of her marriage to Mr. Baylor.

Sylvia, Karen's older sister greeted us with hugs and talked briefly about her parents' remarriages. After the repast, like Chotahs, we talked about the good memories and how nothing and no one could destroy our spiritual connection, our sister-hood. What was not apparent at the time was that we would soon face more death and disease that would challenge and change everything.

That day in 1987, after Nae had been admitted to the hospital, when I arrived and found parking, it was after six. When I reached her floor and did not find her in her room, I went to the nurses' station.

"I am here to see Ms. Douglass."

A young thin nurse sat at a corner desk, her eyes fixed on a computer screen; she looked up at me. "What's your name?"

"Maria, Maria Sourcream. I want to see Ms. Douglass, room 426."

With sympathetic eyes, she said softly, "I am sorry to tell you your friend has expired. Ms. Douglass passed earlier this morning; she left directives to inform you in the event she succumbed to her advanced stages of Sarcoidosis—her lungs."

"You mean she couldn't breathe?"

"Yes. I have some literature that you can read, and you can see her if you'd like." She picked up the receiver and I barely heard her ask for Mike to come to the nurse's station to escort a friend downstairs. A tall African American young man with a goatee and caramel-colored complexion appeared before me. Not knowing what to expect, I looked up at the young fellow.

"What must I do?"

"Come with me. She's in the morgue." He proceeded to the elevators and pushed the down arrow. We entered together and rode down in silence. In the basement, we turned left. The morgue was at the end of a long hallway, double doors closed up the silver drawers inside. Mike checked the placard on the front of one of four waist level drawers. He looked down at me.

"Ready?"

Still I had no idea what to do, what to expect, but I nodded and watched his hand go to the handle and pull.

Except for an ashen look to her skin, Nae appeared like herself lying in the drawer. But dreadfully, her face was contorted like she was about to say something. I stepped back and nodded this time to indicate that was my friend. I heard rather than saw the drawer close. We went back the way we had come except on the trip back, I thought mainly about how devastating it was to lose her. In addition to the lump in my throat, I felt anger toward the perceived ignorance in general about Sarcoidosis, and in particular my powerlessness in helping her fight it.

Returning to the nurse's station, I took the literature she had offered, and somehow made it to my car. With my head resting on the top of the steering wheel, I let the tears flow. I sobbed on and on until I reached in my bag for the paper I took from the nurse. Glancing at the pamphlet, I felt this was all I had to begin to understand Nae's struggle. I vowed to learn all I could to help me accept what happened.

Disease took my friend during her short hospital stay that seemed routine; routine because the uncontrollable coughing associated with Sarcoidosis, the disease I was made aware of after-the-fact, had frequently sent her to the hospital for emergency treatment. She was thirty-two.

After NaeNae made her transition, then mental illness settled in on my girl, Quenchetta. Unlike Nae, Quenchetta refused medical treatment, and it became increasingly challenging to communicate with her.

On one of my many visits to the home they shared, Quenchetta's mother, as usual, opened the front door. When she saw me, she came toward me while pulling the inside door closed. In hushed tones, on the porch, she talked for a few minutes about her observations of the illness.

"She acts like a homeless person. She carries loads of her belongings with her daily and travels around for hours carrying heavy bags. I don't know where she goes with all that stuff, or who she is with all day. I also do not know what she does and she won't tell me. Come on in and see if she'll talk to you." She led me into the house, then nodded in the direction of the kitchen.

"Hey, Chotah," I said, as I walked over to the chair she sat in by the window right before the kitchen door. She looked up. I saw distant eyes, and a paranoid friend.

Quietly, she rose from the chair, glanced around and ushered me into the kitchen. Watching me intensely through glassy eyes, she brought her forefinger to pursed lips and whispered. "My family is not to be trusted."

"Oh," I said. "Maybe you need a little break from them. Let us make a date for lunch, maybe with some of our friends from school."

She scowled. I sensed she might be leery of my intentions. She darted her eyes and compulsively wiped the counter top with a dish cloth.

"Next time," she said. Then, remembering Raoul, with a smile, she asked how he was doing. The corners of my mouth turned upward as I sat down in the chair just inside of the kitchen. We sat together for a little more than a half hour until I got up to leave. Quenchetta followed me all the way to the porch outside.

At the curb, I looked back.

"I'm going to hold you to 'next time' like you said, about lunch soon."

She nodded, gazing as I departed.

"Every time I visited Quenchetta, I just felt overwhelmed." I told Ditmar I thought it was heartache. Seeing Quenchetta like she was, suspicious, fidgety, it made me feel some kind of way. I felt remorseful about being here and my Chotahs being gone. Later, I read about survivor's guilt.

"Seeing death and disease up close was crushing me. Mashing me like a corset. Try as I might, I found it difficult to move forward toward acceptance. Feeling like this forced me to reach back as my mama had told me—for that second gear. She said it was there behind me. But as parenting and work responsibilities took more of my time, when I had a quiet moment, I found it easier to think about the best years the Chotahs had together. And then I began to convince myself to draw strength from them.

"It took a little more than two years after Nae passed in '87 to feel it was possible to find something positive in the loss of all my Chotahs. To develop interest again. And to convince myself that the loss may be a blessing I couldn't grasp, because I couldn't see it. By last Christmas, the distance created by my impending divorce was a motivating factor to move forward. And there was something I felt I just had to do in honor of the Chotahs. I had to affirm still being here in my right mind. But I had to do a lot of talking. I'd say to myself, *Get yourself together, girl. You can do what you want to. You can do it. What about the Chotahs being your spiritual means of defense? Could they be your guardian angels?*"

Ditmar turned toward me, patted my thigh lightly and smiled. Then she posed a question.

"My Mama always said, ain't nothing wrong with talking. Besides me, who else you talking to?" She had been looking out the window as day turned into dusk. Yawning, she pulled a shawl over her shoulders.

"I was talking to a friend from Lincoln University, who recommended some of these readings." I lifted the book off my lap. "There's some real interesting information here." I scanned the cover of *Souls of Black Folk* by W.E.B. DuBois. "In the first half of the twentieth century, all this information was available about our African American condition. And I didn't know."

Ditmar turned toward me and smiled. "Me neither," she said.

"I am thinking, if I take one step, read one book at a time on what's affirming for us, I can return to my first love: reading three to four books a week. That will help me get back in school and turn the guilt I feel into something productive. I know I need to get into that second gear Mama had been telling me about. I gotta just do it."

"And then what?"

"After reading several texts by and about African Americans, I would apply to graduate school. Learn how to change some things in our communities. And reading can keep me from thinking too much about my personal losses, including Kevin's dwindling presence in our boys' lives. Over the past two years, I finally understood his constant absence was due mostly to what I suspected was addiction. I mean, he drank, but I reasoned he had to be doing more than drinking, specially after I found a stash of drugs hidden in the basement. But, there was a part of me that didn't want to accept he got himself involved with unsavory characters and took that trip down crack lane. Precariously, I had faced going down that path with him, and taking the boys with me, or making a break from him for good. The latter took a lot of courage and strength I didn't know I had.

"When I took Kevin to court, I found myself contending with his female African American attorney, who seemed set on using the legal system to frustrate and wear me down. I did not want to believe that I had to have the court system tell my children's father that he had to give me child support and a divorce. And because I was the primary breadwinner, I couldn't afford the kind of lawyer needed in family court. So I used a university law student with limited experience. On the other hand Kevin had free legal services provided by the Philadelphia School Board Worker's union. This was because he drove school buses after he lost his job with the city.

"I don't know if it was that I was so worn down, but it looked as if Kevin's shrewd lawyer, Ms. Thing, was winning more regard from the judge. And I didn't want to fight anymore, so I made a deal to give Kevin the savings we had in turn for the property we owned. That was costly and held long reaching consequences. Like not being able to go back to school while also paying my bills."

"So what are you thinking?" Ditmar asked me. "Going back to school ain't cheap. I'm still paying school loans."

"You preaching to the choir. But I need to know more about how to make things better than I found them in my own community. That's culture. When Mama said get some culture, she was talking about education, reading, playing instruments. I want to study the cultural environments I find myself in, in the city. I have to know I can make a change, change my thinking first."

"What about scholarships?"

I grinned at the idea. "That's what I pray about. And I know all things are possible through prayer." I looked over at Ditmar.

She pursed her lips and glanced down at my book.

"What does DuBois say about how to make change?"

Smiling, I responded, "He says it starts with our thinking. Finding out why we think about ourselves the way we do, inferior to others. He says we show this in our behavior, the way that we seek to honor everything Greek. The way we embrace European ideals like straight hair. I understood from DuBois that we live in a culture that defines us negatively. That's how we begin believing it. We are saturated with media images that affirm this. He says many of us lack the knowledge that confirms Africa as the birthplace of humanity. Basically he is saying, know thyself, which is a common thread in the writings of Malcolm, Frederick Douglass, and on the whole, James Baldwin. That thread made me want to keep reading."

"Uh huh."

"Reading could help with outing the hurt from loss I'm holding onto. I'm still feeling pain that came with seeing death at an early age, up close. That ain't natural. And death and disease including addiction can settle inside you. Eating healthy is only a start to get it out."

"You ain't never lied. Getting healthy is what it's going to take to make real change. We know how hard it is to commit to a couple of days at the gym or to get a short walk on," Ditmar mused. I am sure she was thinking about our brisk walks on break.

I said, "It's both physical and spiritual. My prayer is for health and strength. And it can't hurt to add a little prayer for the money for graduate school for me and maybe music lessons for the boys. That may take some of the stress from them, and get me to a better place.

"I had always envisioned myself a well-educated person. But when I was told our history, we were described as slaves. It made me cringe. Didn't know what I was really feeling. Didn't realize there was more to the story or another version, but as a youngster, I knew I didn't feel right about being described as a slave. It was much later that I learned what it meant to be culturally dislocated. That was when I put a name to what I had felt.

"I think that is what a hallowed truth is. It's sacred. Respected. Like our ancestors. And so it is reasonable to believe that within hallowed truth lies the reality of folks near and dear to us—those that more closely resemble us."

"You mean like our own people?"

"Yes, our people are connected to Africa, where enslaved Africans were jettisoned into African Americans—it's confusing, yet respected. Like raising children. It's complicated, yet valuable."

"That makes sense. We know very little about us, but yet it's important to find out. We might be surprised at what knowing can do for us. What you waiting on?" Ditmar asked.

"God's grace. I need Her blessing. Permission. I have prayed about this. Now I am waiting. We gon' have a ball, and then I will get further into position to receive my blessing." I opened my book to the dog-eared page.

And as dusk rolled into darkness, the train roared ahead. Ditmar and I settled into a quietness that before had escaped us. She nudged me, and I inhaled, then looked up. Raoul came toward us.

He said, "Mom, can I get our sandwiches and blankets from your bag now?" He stood with his weight shifted on one leg, waiting for my response after I exhaled.

"Yes son. Thank you for taking good care of your brother. After you eat and rest a while, it won't be long before we get there. You all need to take a break from reading and the handheld games. Did you figure out the first thing we can all do together when we get there?"

He leaned down, reaching into the bag on the floor between the seats. Finding what he was looking for, he straightened up.

"Yeah, we'll go on Space Mountain."

"Why'd you pick that one?"

"Because it is the most impressive ride, according to the critics. After that, we can take it easy and see some of the less remarkable stuff."

I turned to Ditmar as Raoul returned to his seat more jubilant than I had seen him in a long while.

"What you think?"

"I'm down for 'most impressive.' We can start off with what he says is the loftiest ride. Let all the built up tension out, and then bring it down to a more comfortable level. Like exercise. We build our heart rate up to maximum levels, and then we cool down. I say we go for it. Take things to the rim of our comfort zones."

"Okay."

Hours later, we checked into our rooms, and then met in the lobby dressed in shorts and sneakers. The skies were overcast, yet substantial. The coolness of the late afternoon swirled around us. The children were charged up and showed plenty of teeth and gums.

After standing in a long line, the ride attendant sat us two to a car. Ditmar and I rode together as did her girls in the cars behind us. The brothers brought up the rear. The bars across our laps were secured tightly by the attendant. As the cars rolled forward, I hollered out, "Hold on, y'all!"

"Mom, you alright?"

"Breathe, Sourcream."

Not that long after, I sat on a bench, hunched over, winded. Raoul and Ditmar each had a palm on my back. The last thing I remembered clearly was descending down the track with the children behind us laughing loudly. Then total darkness, the kind that feels plastered on. Even with my eyes stretched as wide open as they could go, I could see nothing but total blackness. I gripped the bar that held us in the car and let out a scream. Then I was on the bench.

"What happened?" I asked, as I exhaled, and began to relax.

"You were screaming and yelling, 'Oh, Lord, help us hold on,'" Raoul said.

"Yeah, you tensed up and screamed. I couldn't tell what was going on, but you may have held your breath too long and then you went limp," said Ditmar.

The girls were watching me with a fretful look on their faces.

"I'm doing better now?"

"Yes!" the children said in unison.

"What about you, Ditmar?"

"I was not expecting that at all, but I'm okay. Let's get something to drink."

I rose from the bench and said, "Whew, I didn't think we could hold on, and I couldn't see nothing. I didn't know what was happening 'cept we were going so fast, I think I did hold my breath. Won't be doing that again."

Chuckling, we walked toward the concession stand together.

I cupped my hands to my mouth and whispered to Ditmar. She turned toward me and the children walked a little ways ahead. We paused.

"I believe I'm ready for life's next chapter. I have faith and that's enough. I was so scared on that ride, but I'm fine now. I couldn't see a thing. All I could feel was darkness. I could hear laughter, children's voices, but I couldn't make out what was being said. Since it felt like I was about to be tossed over the side, I was hoping and praying that didn't happen to the children. I said, 'Lord, please help us to hold on.'

"I called on my Lord. And, at that moment, God provided the means to sustain me in my panicked state. I must have been shocked into suspension. I couldn't hold on, on my own. Fear overtook me. But it's not about fear, it's about faith. It's about trust. Nothing can come between that."

I balled my right hand and moved it toward Ditmar's extended fist. As our fists bumped, smiles touched our eyes. I knew I would be okay, although my heart was still beating a little fast. My time away was a good thing. It helped me to reflect. The guilt I carried came to pass, not to stay. My divine favor made accepting this, among other things, possible. It was God's grace that allowed me in this time, at this place, to be whom I ought to be. A Chotah. I was called to fight the good fight, finish the course, and surrender my experience.

Afterthought:

This story of faith, similar to other stories, offers a basis for comparison. It has been stated, for sure, there are not nearly enough stories about Black life. And fewer can be regarded as 'equalizers.' Some may have had the opportunity to view texts that could be considered equalizing. One is the movie, *The Great Debators*, and another is *Rabbit Proof Fence*. *The Help* is another possibility.

These movies are also about faith; they embrace the views of the folks they are centered on, Black folks. They scream, 'impossible.' But they also have a spiritual component, and that may be the part of Black life that binds Black folk together.

That spiritual factor may render all people to faith. Though, it may not be a bad idea to add a little yoga in the mix.

This is because physical and spiritual health are intertwined; health is crucial to the realities of life, particularly Black life. Truth is, Black folks have largely been on the receiving end of unjust acts, have legally been denied the right to read, and have existed in segregated communities, residential and educational, forever, it seems. All of this while suffering from major illnesses in disproportionate numbers, compared to other groups. Many suffer high levels of stress that come with daily living, not to mention major challenges to accessing proper medical care. This is why faith and being Black seem to go hand-in-hand. Being Black means doing the impossible and the impossible is what Blacks have been doing all along. We've come this far by faith.

So Here We Go Again

RAHEEM SAT IN THE middle of the back seat with the safety belt across his chest. Roughly thirty-six inches tall in sneakers, lightweight with a mahogany skin tone, he was wearing his Philly's baseball cap, holding his electronic gadget as he looked in the direction of the police officer. That morning he had cajoled me into wearing the cap of his home team that had just won the 1980 World Championship.

After teaching three classes at the University's Center City campus in the Lit Brothers Building on 8th, and picking Raheem up from Kindercare on 7th Street right off of Arch Street, I navigated my car around the detour on 7th Street, making my way toward the Vine Street Expressway. At Race Street, the traffic pattern merged into one lane and slowed significantly as it curved to the left onto Vine. I glanced in the rearview at Raheem transfixed on his PI system. *He just loves that thing*, I thought. Looking straight ahead, I inched my way toward the expressway ramp. Then I felt, rather than saw, something like wooden boards underneath. Felt like some sort of makeshift bridge under my tires. *Are they making some kind of road repair here or something? I mused.*

At the entrance to the expressway ramp, the bumper-to-bumper traffic became two lanes, and I used my turn signal to ease my vehicle left. Descending the ramp at the height of rush hour, I noticed several people carrying baggage and other personal belongings. They looked like the people from the downtown shelters. During the day, the folks, who resided in the shelters, were often observed walking around town, or searching in trash bins for a meal or for whatever else they might find. They often looked disheveled or mumbled incoherently and always carried loads of things.

They were hunched over walking in clusters along the left side wall that encased the expressway ramp. Then from the traffic jam, out of nowhere came a thin brown woman pedestrian, trailed by two other women, who drifted right into the left lane in front of my car. I blew my horn and inched slowly behind the women, who ignored me, and continued walking in front of the car. The woman, who came into my view last, blocked the other two, who walked in front of her, but I could see their loose clothing billowing out on the sides. I continued blowing the horn when Raheem looked up from his PI and asked, "What's the matter, Mommy?"

"Something is wrong with this woman; she won't move over."

"Go 'round."

"I can't yet, but if I can just ease into the flow of traffic at the end of this ramp, I will get around her, and hit it." At a snail's pace, I leaned up on the steering wheel, waiting for my chance to merge onto the freeway.

At approximately three hundred feet from the point where the ramp traffic emptied onto the expressway, the small woman directly in front of me stopped walking, bringing the traffic in the left lane to a halt.

"What the—" I called out.

The woman lay down on the road. Amid the commotion, her other two comrades stopped and peeked over their shoulders. Then I, along with several motorists whose cars were behind mine, exited our vehicles. We moved around to the front of my car.

With my heart racing, I breathed in and out deeply, wondering how to defuse the already escalated situation. Then I heard the distant sirens. I thought the police would be descending on the area around the entrance to the Vine Street Expressway any minute.

"Are you hurt?" I asked the woman, who remained lying on the ground with her eyes closed.

The woman's two comrades remained silent, staring down at their fallen friend. They appeared quite calm given the seriousness of the situation. Besides the billowy clothes they wore, on their heads they had on what looked like a burka or gele. Their attire resembled Muslim garments as their heads were covered, and all but their eyes were exposed.

One of the other drivers, a business man in shirt and tie, glanced over at me and hunched his shoulders. He had a deep indentation in the center of his forehead. A woman who had also exited her car, hands on thick hips, implored the fallen woman to explain the situation. She leaned over the woman and said, "Do you need some help, Miss?"

Nothing...not one of the three seemed to have a clue. That or they didn't care. Not one of them spoke at all. The one woman still laid motionless in front of my car, folks hovering over her. She moaned, her arms folded across her middle.

A police cruiser pulled up at the bottom of the ramp and began easing its way alongside the ramp, going in the direction against the arrested vehicles. When the cruiser was close, the two officers in the front seats exited and began to ascend the ramp. As they got closer, gapers who had increased in numbers began to move outward, yielding to the air of authority that blew in with the arrival of the men in blue.

The two associates of the woman lying on the ground observed the cruiser, clasped their hands together in solidarity, huddled simultaneously, and began to pray. I thought, *These women want nothing to do with these policemen, or are they Highway Patrol?*

Wearing thick, knee length boots, hands on their swinging nightsticks, the two uniformed police officers approached. One, a dark-haired thin man with motorcycle sunglasses asked the same questions that I, and the other motorists, had inquired of the woman lying on the ground.

"Ma'am, are you hurt? What's your name?"

She said nothing; just remained horizontal, staring skyward. The officer turned toward me. "What's your name, Ma'am?"

As I took it all in, I peered suspiciously at him. *I believe I have encountered his type before.*

"Jamila Rivers," I replied. He and his partner appeared the sort that would belong to the good-old-boys club. That type that often talked down to others in an attempt to appear like a big shot.

The officer asked, "What happened?"

I said, "This woman sauntered into the traffic with her accomplices and fell in front of my car, Sir."

He walked over to the other two women while speaking into his shoulder device.

"We need an ambulance at the entrance to Vine Street Expressway at Eighth." Then he said something to the accomplices. They said something back, but I could not hear.

"How are you doing, young fellow?" said the other officer as he looked into the rear passenger window of my car. He was thin, blond, and had a bushy blond mustache.

What is he up to? I thought. Automatically, I felt distrust since past experiences with Philadelphia police had been negative.

The other officer was still speaking with the accomplices; he looked down and wrote something on a pad.

Raheem looked up at the officer who spoke to him; he pointed his thumb to his chest and said, "I'm good, but my mommy had a hard time getting around that lady." He strained his neck to the left, trying to get a look at the woman, who still lay on the ground moaning.

The officer asked, "Is your mommy a good driver?"

Raheem replied, "Yes."

With my arms crossed over my chest, leaning against the driver side front bumper of my car, I asked, "Is there a problem, Officer?"

He looked up at me and then back down at Raheem.

I said, "May I ask your name, Officer?"

Walking toward the rear of my vehicle, the officer turned back, flicked his thumb toward his partner and said, "Ask him my name."

I looked in the direction of the approaching siren-blazing ambulance, as the officer who had spoken into his shoulder device directed traffic onto the expressway and west down Vine Street. Then both officers approached me as I remained leaning against the front bumper of my car, blocking Raoul's view.

The blond said, "Ma'am, we may have to take you downtown for questioning."

I said, "Take *me* downtown? Why? By the way, I didn't get your name." I looked directly at the white officer who glanced first toward the expressway and then back at me without saying a word. The other officer then spoke.

"Miss, may we see your license and registration?"

"Absolutely. And what is your name, Officer?" I asked him.

"My name is Officer Bradley and my partner here is Officer Moore. We just need to take you in to the station and ask a few questions. Is there someone you can call to come and get your son?" He accepted my documents and looked down at them.

"I don't understand. The woman obviously is participating in some kind of scam; she laid down right in front of my car at the height of rush hour and you want to take me in? What is the problem?"

"Miss," Officer Bradley continued. "We are not sure of what happened here; the witnesses indicate you hit the woman with your car. We will need to bring you in and ask a few questions. Now rather than be handcuffed and taken downtown, would you like to call someone to come for your son? Then we can get the questioning over with while the woman is transported to Hahnemann Hospital."

"I do not have anyone to call for my son. He will have to come with me. And please be sure to consult with your superiors on the matter to avoid harassing the wrong person. Since I sit on the bench in Philadelphia, I could make a major decision about your career."

Both officers looked at each other and the blond whispered something I could not hear. They walked around my car; one checked my credentials while the other radioed in my driver's license and ran my plate. The dark-haired officer came over to me, handed over my credentials and said in an angry tone, "Which bench do you sit on?"

I looked at him. "Ask your superior."

Flushed, Officer Bradley's expression hardened. I knew I had angered him. He turned to go join his partner in the squad car as he was speaking into the car radio. Both officers approached me again. I was still leaning against my front bumper when Officer Bradley said, "We have decided to let you go, Miss Rivers. If we have further questions, we may be contacting you later regarding this incident." He joined his partner in the cruiser with the lights flashing on top. Both officers sat there, looking down as if writing something.

Relieved it had worked again, I thought about how I had avoided all the hoopla that could go along with being taken downtown—with navigating police personnel that do not always regard citizens with respect, those who resemble me anyhow. The workers reading me wrong: a haughty Black woman in a power position. If they sensed I was too proud, they could cause more problems for me. *Anyway, by the time they spend their time figuring out who employs me and how high on the echelon my position goes, this matter will have passed; I am just happy they're letting me go.*

I put my credentials in my pocket and moved toward the driver's side door.

I felt somewhat vindicated for all the times officers like Moore had intimidated folks who looked like me and gotten away with it. I was just a bit concerned about perpetrating a fraud to avoid going downtown. How that could cause me problems in the future. But, I could not help feeling a bit justified. I would deal with repercussions, if any, later.

Despite feeling a tiny sense of guilt at my portentousness, I could not resist reacting to the officers' decision to let me go. So, I opened my car door, got inside, and while fastening my seat belt, I turned toward the back and smiled at Raoul who sat patiently. When I turned back around, I nodded toward the two officers as I began my descent onto the Vine Street Expressway and I said in a lighthearted tone, "Good decision, officers; have a great evening."

Family Matters

FOR THE PAST MONTH, her mother had been planning to go visit her best friend, Tammi Reid, Sammi's wife. After Sunday Service when she stopped by Emily's for a bite to eat, she asked, "You feel like going down to Tammi's after we're finished?"

Emily nodded as she took in that deliberate look her mother gave her that could not be denied. It was Mrs. Green's way of making her intention known that she planned on getting her way. Now that their friend had the big "C," Emily knew she would eventually go, but didn't feel much like driving. She knew she had to go visit on account of Mrs. Tammi was her friend, too.

Sitting at the kitchen table and watching a cooking show on the small television that sat at the back of the table had become their after church routine. Mrs. Green, a small-built widow with a lot of spunk, stood only four feet eight inches and weighed less than one hundred five pounds. She seemed to dominate their relationship.

Her dutiful daughter, Emily, stood five-foot-two, almost doubling her mother's weight. While Mrs. Green put the dishes in the pan in the sink, Emily rose to go get her jacket and the car keys from the dining room where she had placed both when she came in the front door earlier.

Mrs. Green grabbed her hat off the chair beside the radiator, and swung her pocketbook up on her shoulder. "You ready?" she said. She pushed in her chair, preparing to go out the back door. Emily appeared in the kitchen doorway, her lips pressed together.

"Let's go."

They walked out the back door, got in the car, and with Emily at the wheel, they turned right out of the driveway. Another right at the light and they proceeded down Ogontz Avenue. Humming softly, Emily stared straight ahead in her recently purchased brand new black 1985 Renault 18i.

Rather than go uphill toward Philadelphia's Route One Expressway south, they drove in silence down Belfield Avenue, over Stenton going south, veered left toward Roberts Avenue and proceeded on down to Fox Street. Emily's eyes were on the road and Mrs. Green sat stoically riding shotgun. Emily thought uneasily about seeing the Reids. *Mrs. Tammi sure do love Mr. Sammi. Poor thing.*

Big and bald, Sammi was a boisterous man, friend, and former neighbor. He had an infectious smile and, according to word on the street, an insatiable penchant for young women. Other things said included that Mr. Sammi gambled. His physique resembled a snowman, he was loud, and he loved good food and drink. But he was always showboating. His friends rallied around him since he could put out a spread. Only thing, it was Mrs. Tammi doing all the fixings—Sammi taking all the credit.

Sammi came from a family of five brothers, all big. Their weight was such an issue that it took about a dozen pallbearers

to lift Ralph's, Sammi's older brother's casket. Besides their large-
ness were their even bigger egos.

Emily asked, "What did her girls have to say about her condition?" She was thinking about the cancer that had invaded Mrs.
Tammi's body and the reaction, if any, that her three daughters
may have shared. The youngest of the Reid's daughters worked at
the Girard Bank with Mrs. Green.

Mother reported, "Jacki told me her sister would call me.
Haven't talked to Mimi. Vivian said Tammi was in good spirits,
but we had better come to see her soon, s'all she said."

"Did she say anything about Mr. Sammi?" asked Emily.

"Like what? All Tammi ever mentioned was that she knew
about Sam's escapades and Vivian knows that already."

"Is that what's making Mrs. Tammi sick—worrying about
what he's up to?"

"Who, Sammi? Is that what you think? She has an illness,
doesn't mean she's any more worried about him than usual.
Why?"

"I just always thought she became sick so suddenly, and
I began to think about what all Mrs. Tammi knows about his
dealings."

"I don't think she knows about all his dealings, but she knows
enough. She does know he has girlfriends out there. Her children
know, too, but they try to keep some of that mess from their
mother. He ought to be ashamed."

"He ain't shame," said Emily. "I told him when he came into
the County Assistance Office with that little girl who was eighteen

years old, that *she* was not eligible for food stamps and he gon' tell me my job. When I looked at Mr. Sammi, I was ashamed. Always viewed him as a respectful man in the community, being married to Mrs. Tammi and all. I wanted him to know that I knew exactly what he was up to and that regardless of what he thought, the young lady, baby or no baby, was not eligible for food stamps period."

"He got loud on you in the office, did he?"

"Yeah. And he thought he could make demands, creating a scene. Ms. Watson at the desk said, 'Emily you have a live one in the **District Office**. Come on out here and resolve it.' I was cool as a cucumber. When he recognized me, he stood his ground for his baby momma. Poor thing, she was nothing but a baby herself. I read him his rights though and got them both out of there. Poor Mrs. Tammi, she don't deserve that. Who would have thought?"

"Well, we can't do nothing about what Sammi is up to today. All we can do is visit Tammi. We are not even going to mention it to their girls again. They already know, and besides, they just want to make their mother comfortable."

"Ready?" Emily said as she looked over at her mother then turned the other way reaching for the car door handle. They walked arm-in-arm on the cement pavement up the block, passing porch-front homes where several little children ran up and down playing.

The front of the Reid's house was freshly painted, the porch neatly swept. Mother and daughter ascended the front steps. Emily tried the screen door. It was unlocked.

The corners of Emily's mouth turned up a little at seeing Mrs. Tammi lying in her lounge chair, legs sprawled out, big smile on her face. She used to be a thick woman; now she looked shriveled and despite her smile, very fatigued. The smell of fried chicken filled the house.

Mimi was in the kitchen as usual. At the sound of voices in the living room, she came out with an apron on and kissed Viola Green and then Emily on their cheeks. "How y'all doing? Want some chicken?"

"Naw, service was long and my feet are aching. We gonna just sit and talk to your mom for a minute or two," Emily's mother replied.

"Nothing for me, Mimi, I'm fine. How you doing, girl?"

Mimi had her hand on her hip where her apron hung. Her smile touched her eyes, and she looked at Emily and then at Ms. Vi. "I'm good, Em. You, and Ms. Vi, you both look well."

Mimi was the eldest of three. Thick like her mother used to be, she had big bright eyes and a round face. She was a great cook like most of the other Reids, and Mimi's temperament was easy going and fun loving. Light skinned like her mother and father, Mimi wore her hair short and sassy, which complimented her face as well as her figure. It seemed to finish off her big brick house look with her wide hips and small feet. She didn't take no stuff from nobody, and when it came to her father, she was the buffer between her mother knowing or not knowing the mess people would say about Sammi.

Like her younger sister Vivian, Mimi sang on the church choir and she led the culinary ministry. She also helped with other church functions. Her mother could count on both daughters to prepare Sunday dinner and take care of her affairs.

Emily remembered her former next door neighbor from public housing being a little frailer than the last time she saw her a year ago before the fiasco in the district office with her husband. As a child, after a scolding or punishment from her parents, Mrs. Tammi had offered candy to her. That was when Emily was confined to either the front or back stoop—being allowed to go, as her mother would often declare "no further."

Mrs. Tammi also had a round face, short, pressed to the nine's hair, and keen features just like her eldest daughter. Her skin looked pale and she did not move much in the chaise, but she patted her thigh, inviting Emily to come sit beside her.

Emily bent down and kissed her cheek briefly, brushing her hard arm lightly. She sat on the end of the chaise, watching her own mother out the corner of her eye. Her mother shifted her weight from her left to right foot and exhaled.

"How you doing, Tammi?" Emily's mother said.

"I'm doing a little better since you came to see me and you brought LeLe. Hi, honey," she said, and her eyes gazed at Emily sitting at the end of the chair. She was first to start affectionately calling Emily LeLe, similar to Aretha Franklin's nickname, ReRe.

"Hi, right back at ya. How they treating ya?" Em asked.

"I'm going to be fine, Le. Don't you worry about me." She grimaced as she straightened up. She leaned down and grabbed Emily's face in both her hands and pressed her face to Emily's so that they were nose to nose. They both smiled.

There had always been something special between her and her LeLe. Although Tammi knew Vi tried to manage LeLe's childhood weight, she had still fed Emily between mealtimes. Tammi could burn, as folks would say. And LeLe was privy to those special tastings that often took place in the backyard out of sight of others who would have died to partake in the 'smack-your-momma' dishes Mrs. Tammi made. Her hips and Lele's, both held the telltale signs of good soul food eating.

And that unique relationship they held, served as a spiritual bond that seemed solid as a rock. This showed in the way that Emily stroked Tammi's outstretched leg, and the way she hummed Tammi's favorite hymn, "Amazing Grace." It was that type of connection Emily wanted to hold on to.

Less than one month later, it appeared that last visit gave Tammi a sort of strength she needed to put up a brave front. This seemed so because not long after that visit, Mrs. Tammi passed. She slipped away in her sleep and the church shouted with joy. No more suffering. No more pain.

A few weeks after Mrs. Tammi passed, while sitting at the table eating, Mr. Sammi had a heart attack. A day later in the hospital, he passed away. Again, the church shouted with joy. Some thought the elation was for Sammi, but there were others who thought the good Lord had bestowed favor upon Mrs. Tammi by taking her home first. Their children and the other funeral goers were left to process the calamity at Sammi's home-going services.

At the funeral, Vivian, the middle daughter surveyed the congregation. She had skin the color of oak, and she appeared sturdy. She was about five feet eight inches tall with intense brown eyes. Mr. Sammi's body lay just beneath the podium from which she spoke.

"First giving honor to God and church leaders," Vivian, began to pray. "Oh Lord, how merciful is thy name. Please bless us this day, a day we have never seen before, and allow us to heal from our misgivings. Have your way today, Lord, and let us lean not unto our own understanding, but trust in You from whence all blessings flow. Amen."

To a church filled with onlookers, and with Mr. Sammi laid out in front of the congregation in a navy suit and gold coffin, Vivian began again, "At this time, we want to acknowledge the family of Sammi Reid, my father and a friend to many of you. Although necessary, my mother may not have understood what I am about to do. Nevertheless, Jacki, MiMi, and I realize that it is time. Will all the children of the late Sammi Reid please stand."

Emily, her mother, and a few neighbors from the projects who were in the same pew could hardly refrain from turning their heads toward the rear of the church. That was where the noise of many shuffling feet came. Then Ms. Ethel, a dark skinned round woman who sat to the left of Emily turned toward the back. She had on a hat like the one Celie wore in the *Color Purple* and a flowered smock. Out of the corner of Emily's eye, she saw Ms. Ethel's mouth agape. Then others began to turn and look. All around the small hot packed church, people were fanning themselves and staring at the folks standing.

When Emily turned around to look, folks were still rising, joining the almost twenty or more already standing.

Staring at the standing folks in the church, Vivian said, "Will you all please come to the front?" At the altar, the group gathered in a circle and Vivian prayed. "Lord, bless this gathering. Lord, heal us at this time from all the misgivings of my earthly father. Bless those standing here today and those who did not stand, but belong to Sammi Reid. Lord, bring us together in a way that is pleasing in Your sight, and keep us connected as we begin to regard one another under Your guidance. Direct our paths, Lord, that we may come to an understanding of who we are in Your sight. Grant us mercy, Lord, as we try to move beyond what it looks like here, to what we can become as a family. Thank you, Lord, bless my mother's soul, and God bless my father's journey. Amen."

After the folks who stood up front returned to their seats, Vivian eulogized her father. She spoke for about ten minutes. A prayer of comfort was led by a church deacon. A congregational hymn was sung, and there was a silent reading of the obituary. Then, the pallbearers were directed up front to prepare for the interment.

After they carried out the coffin, the congregants filed past the family on the front row, shook their hands, and offered condolences. Emily, her mother, and Ms. Ethel hugged the three daughters, and kissed each lightly on their cheeks. There were few dry eyes in the sanctuary.

As the visitors filed out of the little church and proceeded to their cars, Ms. Ethel asked Emily if she and her mother were going to the cemetery. Several people got in their cars with hazard lights on to accompany the body to its final resting place.

"No," said Emily.

"Can you drop me off, Em?"

"No problem."

Emily's mother got in the car up front, and Ms. Ethel rode in the back. Emily drove slow and all said very little. Ms. Vi looked down at the obituary she held on her lap. Then she looked out the window and signed. She said, "That was something else."

"Yes it was," said Ms. Ethel.

"I have never witnessed a service like that," said Emily.

"I don't think anyone else has either," said Emily's mother Vi.

"Sammi left all that for his family to deal with. That's a shame," said Ms. Ethel.

Emily's mother nodded her head; she pressed her lips together. The rest of the ride home was in silence and the mood was somber.

"Have a good afternoon, Ms. Ethel. Tell everyone hello for me," said Emily as Ethel exited the car.

"Thank you. I will."

"Lord, well ain't that something?"

"Yes, Mother, that was a trip."

"What we gon' do with our folks?"

"Love 'em. Keep on loving 'em."

"When we gon' do better?"

"When Jesus come."

"That'll be too late."

"That's the point. You coming over or you want me to drop you off?"

"Take me home. I can't get over what happened today."

"When you think our family has ridiculous issues to deal with, think about those siblings in that church today. Not much can compare."

"I think I'll keep my family."

"You had better. You can't trade family, although that's a thought."

"Alright daughter, talk to you later." Emily's mother got out of the car, and waved goodbye.

Both mother and daughter had shared that story to disbelieving listeners. It was on the lips of those who witnessed the shocking service for months after Sammi was buried. No doubt, he left a long lineage as well as a lasting impression.

If God Tarries

AFTER MY DISCHARGE FROM the US Air Force in '64, I resided in West Philly until 1969 when I rented an apartment in Germantown. G-town, in Northwest Philly, was thought of as a place where bourgeois Blacks lived. This could have been due to the large number of light-skinned blacks residing there. Don't know, but it didn't matter. I had to get away from my girl, Sharmel, and her demands. Most of our hassles were about her intent on getting married. This was her idea when we graduated high school and I left for the service.

I should have said I wasn't ready, but when I completed my tour, it took me five years to realize I wanted something else. One thing I wanted was to be able to drink in peace without a lotta nagging. Finding one of them G-town girls couldn't be worse than Sharmel, with her no-drinking, go-to-church-on-Sunday attitude. It was my idea that women needed to stay in their place, that a good woman would learn this over time with a little convincing from a good man. This opinion, based on assurance from my worldly father, I never saw any reason to change.

There was a particular woman, however, who did not fit into my notions, but caught my fancy anyway. The summer of '72, when I turned twenty-eight, I met Lula Mae Clark. She was only sixteen at the time, though she claimed she was legal. My background in security led to the truth of the matter the winter of that year. But by then, her brick house measurements had me whipped. After going out with her discreetly for four years, Lula Mae agreed to settle down and have a baby. Thirteen years later, we were married. Eight years before that, in '77, we had Oscar, Junior.

Lula Mae was a quick study and mature for her age, so it wasn't easy for me to convince her that I would lead, and she would follow. Eventually, I discovered that more maturity settled in on her with the birth of Junior, and that made me feel like I needed to keep close watch on her. Parenthood seemed to grow her. She was constantly reading and planning ways to work in the public sector.

Eventually, Lula found time to resume her education and balance the roles of office clerk and mother. While I worked security jobs and tried to keep an eye on her as much as possible, her momma and her sister provided the instruction she sought in raising Junior and, to my dismay, eventually, Lula graduated college and began teaching. Her interest spread to community advocacy, while the extent of my attention was mainly enjoying the nightlife. The nightlife led to increased drinking, which led to unaddressed depression and then to drugs. I just needed to numb the pain of depression a little, and drugs were easy to access. It was not until much later that I grappled with the world of hurt that that choice caused.

1999 – Philadelphia, Pennsylvania

OSCAR, JUNIOR, LIKE THE other males in Lula Mae's family, was thought to be depressed. Twenty-two years ago when Junior was born, folks had depression. I mean, young men were dealing with the aftermath of Vietnam and all. Now it seems if it ain't claims of folks being bipolar, they depressed. Especially among Black folks. When asked about causes of depression they'd likely say, "Pick one."

Lula Mae said, "Oscar, Junior had a lot to be depressed about."

She was always analyzing things. Junior had a job. He was in school. What he needed was a good woman. What else was there?

To that she said, "Look at how the overall lack of jobs and the weak economy has created a bad situation for African American males, less likely than other groups to have an active father in their lives. Something is wrong with that picture."

We were sitting in the kitchen of our row home that I had worked hard to secure. Before, we often had coffee at the table while looking at the garden beyond the patio out back. That was then. Now, she took care of the vegetable garden that had been my passion. She kept it up. But, the woman was a pain. Why she have to go get too deep on me? We were talking about our son. Then she babbled on about all kinds of things. *What made her always want to look at the negative?*

She went on. "Jobs once held by men are held by women now."

Well Lula was right about that. This was by design, according to some Black folks. The thing was, Lula Mae didn't stop there. She went on talking about how bad things had gotten while I wanted to just be left alone. According to my wife, "Black folks are moving in reverse, 'cept they don't act like they know it."

Lula wore her thick hair drawn back in a bun, which accentuated her bright eyes. Sexy, with a gap in her front teeth, she was more than a half foot shorter than me. Although she was constantly dieting, she was round and fleshy where it counted.

She said, "With the advent of women's liberation, the proliferation of violence and drugs in the communities, and the overall compromised health of individuals, the result is women heading more African American families than men. Men are succumbing to drugs, going to prison at alarming rates, and sugar diabetes, as well as AIDS, average just about one in four persons of color. Living like this is bad for everybody. It's worse for African American men, the rare ones who beat the odds and live beyond the age of twenty. And if they don't get killed by gun violence, they carry the weight of it all on their shoulders."

Yeah, that was our son, Junior. One of the rare ones. Grown up now, unlike some of his peers who had got caught up in the madness of living while black, but he was still struggling with a lot. Hell, going to school during his primary years with white folks was probably equally, if not more disturbing than what he had to deal with now on city streets; if he could handle going to school with them back then, he could survive much more. He could survive what had his mother worried now. He had survived gun violence so far, and he would keep on surviving it like the rest of us, with or without my active involvement in his life. His mother just needed to stop talking, trying to make me feel guilty.

If she left well enough alone, we could get back together and work from there. Her diatribes made me think she still harbored anger about my lack of involvement with Junior's activities. She acted like I didn't care, didn't feel awkward about his almost drowning at a swim party during his primary years. I know I refused to go to the party out in Bala Cynwyd where his white classmates lived, but Lula Mae had a fit.

That day, she had complained about having to interact with the white parents from his school without me. I didn't want to deal with that. Since she'd sent him to that school, she should have taken him to the school's events, not me. Or she should have said he couldn't go. Anyway, we could have saved some of that private school money. All I had wanted to do was have a few beers, and relax before getting ready to go in to work later.

After that incident, when Junior would not go back in the water, Lula signed him up for a refresher swim course. And when that did not erase his fear, Lula Mae sought counseling for him. She came right out and said, "Junior needs to talk about the declining situation at home and the apparent alcoholism of his father."

I didn't deal with what Lula Mae was saying back then, and now here we were more than a decade later. My drinking had become so bad, I forgot which lies I had told her. Lula wasn't no dummy. She knew just where to find me drinking and doing a little more than that when she drove over to 19th Street the other night to tell me Junior was in the hospital.

My drinking and cocaine use were out of control. Lula knew. And although I never thought she would, four years after we were married, in 1989, she had asked me to leave and go get myself some help.

Lula gazed all around the kitchen. Everywhere but at me. "What you thinking about?" I asked.

She stared at the wall and fiddled with her cup of coffee. Then her gaze shifted toward me and I saw her eyes were moist.

"I was just thinking about the time he got sick before this."

"I remember, he got sick as soon as he went to the university."

In the fall of 1995, during his freshman year at Drexel, Junior was diagnosed with a T-cell disorder. His red and white blood cell development was out of sync—he suffered from extremely high fever and flu-like symptoms. This prevented him from having regular attendance. He had withdrawn from classes, and convalesced at home for more than two months. Unable to say how long his condition would last, the doctors said, "It would have to take its course." For fear of not being able to make up and catch up, he took a leave from school.

Lula said, "Yeah, but he did recover. You remember last winter and all that snow? Junior had two jobs: one at the university and one delivering newspapers at four in the morning. He was also taking night courses. He had been in his second round of counseling for the past two years, and he believed he was making progress."

"Two jobs! Most can hardly keep one. I hope he wasn't taking none of them mental drugs. That's what probably landed him where he is."

"He needed counseling. He trusted his therapist. He also needed you, but you were busy getting high." She sighed, and then stared back at the wall.

"Didn't Junior tell you that counselor had prescribed anti-depression medicine? You had said that the work overload, the stress of school and the influence of the depression medication pushed him to his limits. How come you were so eager to have him see that counselor? What good did it do?"

"I knew he needed counseling. The therapist had confirmed that Junior was a studious fellow who made good grades, but was suffering from an adjustment disorder and confusion from turbulence in his home life as a youngster."

I just looked at Lula, my hands clasped between my knees. I thought, *Junior is a good height, five-ten like me; he don't weigh more than one-eighty like I used to weigh in my twenties, and his skin tone is between his mother's medium and my light brown complexion. He's impeccable. My son. His mother was probably nagging him too much, and he didn't need no counseling, but he must have taken drugs the counselor recommended and he wanted to take himself out.*

Lula asked, "What you thinking about? You think this is about you or his debt?"

I shook my head.

"When Junior moved out, his rent and school loans became unmanageable. Then he came back home. He hadn't been here a month when he began to make demands and obnoxious statements toward me. He would make snide remarks, and he just laughed at me when I asked for his help with chores. His behavior was borderline despicable. I knew the work overload and other daily stressors were a lot for him to handle, but I had to do something." She darted her eyes toward me.

"What'd you do?"

"I asked him to leave, although I did not know where he would go. I was concerned about him, his bizarre behavior, using profanity and his disrespect in general. To protect my own sanity, I put him out. After finishing his paper route and after sleeping in the car in the back of the house in the snow, Junior rang the back doorbell and asked me if I would accompany him to his scheduled counseling session at Chestnut Hill Hospital. He looked tired and glassy eyed, and a little off balance. He seemed to be leaning to one side instead of standing straight. Reluctantly, I opened the door, stepped aside and let him come in. He said the appointment was at ten, so I just went upstairs to get dressed."

"What was he doing while you dressed? Why did he ask you to go with him? He'd been going alone."

"I asked him, 'What made you invite me to the session?' He said, 'I really did not know what to say to you and I didn't think that you would agree to go, but something told me to ask anyhow.' So, I said, 'Let me get dressed and we can go.' Told him he looked sleep deprived and that sleeping in his car in the elements was not a good thing. He said he thought he'd be okay, didn't have anywhere else to go and he had turned on the ignition to keep warm while he caught a few hours of sleep."

"Did he say why he had been disrespecting you?"

"I asked him what did he see as the problem with being disrespectful to me and having to be put out."

"What did he say?"

"He said, 'I don't know why I behaved the way that I did the other night, and I don't know why you have such an effect on me either.'" Lula pursed her lips. She had wrinkles in her forehead.

You probably nagged him to death like you did me. I wish you would just get to the point so that I can go.

Lula said, "Junior went up to the bathroom as I came down dressed and ready to go. I drove the three miles to the hospital while he sat in the front seat with his eyes closed. We parked in the garage adjacent to the out-patient building, and made the trek up the hill toward the medical offices.

"After we got on the elevator that took patients to the second floor bridge level, from there we took the enclosed bridge across to the other side where the medical offices are housed. I noticed signs on the bridge announcing health related classes like smoking cessation, sugar diabetes, and weight loss options.

"From the bridge, I could see parking spaces for the emergency room down below. The landscaping on the hospital grounds looked very nice, and the walls on either side of the medical office's suite were a pale green. I didn't want to look at Junior too much. He dragged his feet, and seemed off balance. Maybe he was looking that way to get sympathy for his situation that he had brought on himself—speaking to me in a nasty tone and using profanity. It was good, though, that Junior invited me to his session. At least he had family with him. He said he felt he needed to resolve some things happening to his family.

"We separated again briefly. When the automatic doors to the suite opened, I saw the bathroom signs and felt a need to go. I told him to go on ahead of me, that I'd be along after I used the rest room.

"When I came out, I opened the first door on the right, and walked into the waiting room of the counselor's office. The receptionist, a young blonde, told me, 'Go right in.' When I entered the door to my left, there was Junior and his counselor, a young thin white man with dark hair and glasses. Junior looked dazed. I got right to the point, and I said, 'As Junior's mother, I am here to support him.' The counselor swiveled around in his chair, and with his back to us, he wrote something down in a hurry. Without turning toward us, while looking down at his notepad, he said something but I could not hear. Then, he tore off the script he was writing and swung around to face us.

"He said, 'It seems Oscar has deliberately taken more medication than prescribed; he should be taken directly to emergency and please give them this information.' He handed me the script, and I took charge."

I had been sitting with drooped shoulders, forearms resting on my thighs, listening to her rant. I reluctantly asked her, "What did you do after you knew he took pills?"

"I glanced at Junior, who seemed even more lethargic than before; although he was sitting down, he appeared off balance. I quickly took his hand and guided him up from the chair and out the door, across the bridge, and down the elevator to the ground level. I didn't fully realize going through the motions of getting to Emergency, but when we arrived and handed the note to the ER attendant, Junior was immediately escorted to a wheelchair and the triage nurse began asking questions: 'What did you take? When? How much?'

"She placed a blood pressure cuff on Junior's arm, and ushered him into the back where the medical staff worked on him. They inserted an IV and put a tube down his throat. Junior was fighting them in slow motion. They told me that they might pump his stomach, depending on the time line of the overdose.

"As it turned out, he didn't have his stomach pumped; the on-call doctor said that the meds that Junior had taken were already well en route so that it was 'wait and see.' He was admitted to the critical care unit where a shunt was placed in his neck to control his airway that had started compressing. I wiped his brow with a cool cloth while looking at his bulging eyes. He seemed afraid, anxious and disoriented all at the same time. I just started praying. That gave me some peace while I sat with our son until he was sedated and fell into a forceful sleep. Every now and again, he seemed to twitch.

"I made my way back to my car in the parking lot and drove home. I had to talk to somebody about what was happening and I didn't know whether I should or could try to reach you. So, I decided to call my father. Dad had tried to end his life at one time. I called my sister, Lottie, and then I called my mother. Finally, I contemplated contacting you. Although I sensed you were in the throes of crack cocaine, I still felt you should share in this calamity. I kept in mind that your irresponsible behavior had taught me not to expect logic."

Truth dawned in her watery eyes. Lula got up and moved over to the stove by the basement door to fix more coffee. Then she sat back down, lit a cigarette, blew out smoke, and stared straight ahead.

I wanted to tell her again that I didn't want her to smoke, but who was I to criticize? I knew what she had said was painful for her. What she had said about me getting high was painful for me, but accurate. Then she looked at me with wounded eyes. Was she letting me stew? I thought about all that had happened, all that I hadn't helped with. Now she insisted that I listen to the whole story of how Junior landed in the hospital.

I had constantly asked her for money when I was not working regularly or trying to help with family obligations. I had told her many stories about how other women helped their man, and she should be more than willing to help me even though I did not appear to be helping myself.

"I don't know what else I can do. I'm staying at Richard's right now, but I want to come home Lula."

"The dots do not connect," she said. Then she mashed out her cigarette.

She noted how I had been put out of my parent's home; how my sister and only brother wouldn't even give me a place to stay, and said my hygiene was slipping. She said something about my station in life not being what it should be, but I knew she loved me.

I said, "You love me, don't you?"

She pressed her lips in a line. Then she exhaled.

"Yes. But the reality of your situation is apparent to everyone else, but you, Oscar, and at times, I even try to rationalize your circumstances without admitting the apparent drug and alcohol abuse. This creates distance between my family members and me. They're tired of hearing about the illogical stunts you pull. Like being at an obvious drug house, but denying drug use. When Lottie told me that I should notify you of Junior's situation, I didn't know what to do. But, I got up and drove over to Richard's house, and I knocked on what's known as the crack house door."

I thought about her going there and what that must have felt, not to mention, looked like. Richard lived in a corner house with crumbling front steps and boarded up windows. The open front porch was barely attached to the house frame and there was no railing, no screen door, and the wooden front door looked beaten and warped like it belonged to an abandoned house.

On the second floor, where I could do my thing, I had raised the window and shouted in response to a knock on the door. "Whose there?"

Lula Mae stepped back off of the porch and away from the front door and looked up. She saw my face, although it was growing dark outside, and I know it must have appeared drawn and small; she saw what I saw in the mirror: sunken hollow looking eyes. Surprised to see her, I noticed the worried look in her eyes. Her face contorted, she dragged on a cigarette. She had a shameful look.

I shouted down to her, "What's wrong?" Lula just shook her head. That's when I shut the window and came downstairs.

"What you said that night at Richard's really shocked me," I said.

"Enough to get help? To hear your son has had some kind of melt down, took pills, and is in the hospital, that's a shocker. But that didn't stop you from asking me for money."

"I had to get to the hospital," I said. I thought about all the times she had denied me.

Lula Mae knew better than to give me money as I had swindled her out of thousands and I was practically living on the street. I am glad she realized that if I could grasp the urgency of the situation, I just might use the money for carfare. I think that's why she gave me the twenty dollars and drove off.

She said, "Good, you got to see some of what I saw, some of what I've had to deal with. I wasn't aware you were in the family room the next morning when I went to Junior's room; he was sweating and tensed, his eyes were bulging. When the nurse asked me to excuse myself because she wanted to administer something to help him calm down, I discovered you were waiting in the room next to the critical care unit. When I saw you, unshaven, wearing a trench coat that looked as if it had not been washed in quite some time, you looked so thin, like you do now. You were hiding behind that baseball cap pulled down over your ears, with your unruly gray hair sticking out from under it. You and Lottie were there drinking coffee."

"Yeah, I got up early the next morning after you came by, and when I got to the hospital, I saw Lottie getting off the elevator. She took me to the family room."

"My sister always had a way with you. That's why she tried to prepare you for what you would see. She was making light talk to help you relax, wasn't she?"

"She did do that. Then you came in asking questions."

"I said 'Hey' to both of you. I was glad to see Lottie and you. I only asked about the smell in the room because it was so strong."

"And I told you. There's no heat where I stay; that was the odor from kerosene that gets in my clothes. Then you wanted to know more."

"I just asked if you had running water."

"Uh huh." *Another inquisition.* I sipped my coffee that had turned cold, and then Lula continued.

"My sister tried to be helpful to all that day. When she said that you and I should go first into Oscar's room ahead of her, she was right. She must have known he couldn't take too much stimulation. That's why she waited while we visited."

"Uh huh, that was some visit." Junior didn't look tensed, as Lula had described. He did have a thick tube in his mouth. Then when he saw me, he appeared to hyperventilate; his eyes got real wide and his chest heaved up and down rapidly. The nurse came in. She put something in his IV. That settled him some, and Lula and I just sat there like we are now. I guess that was good to do—just sit with him. He appeared peaceful when we came out to let Lottie go to his bedside. I leaned in with my forearms on my thighs, and with my head bent, I said, "I wanted to take my own life at times."

Lula just sat staring, letting me absorb all she'd said. I looked at her and thought about Junior at the hospital. It remained on my mind, mingling with the other madness in my life. *Did she even hear what I just said?* I wanted to tell her I was ready to get help with my addiction, but the words were lodged in my throat and I couldn't get them out. Besides, she had so much to think about: her role in Junior's suicide attempt—putting him out; my role; the anti-depressants; and his overall stress of working two jobs and going to school.

Finally, she said, "Since the Lord has kept you here, I can only hope that thinking of suicide was your rock bottom, as I hope Oscar Junior's act of trying it, is his. Folks say you have to get all the way down to get up. If that's true, this event with Junior's 'meltdown' is a beat down and if God tarries, tomorrow will be another chance to get up. To try and set things right. I pray you do. And I hope to see you there tomorrow. It will get better. It has to."

Lula got up and walked over to the back door. She opened it, as I rose and touched her lightly on the shoulder, hoping and praying that I connected with her strength. Then I left.

I walked out onto the patio, past the vegetable patch and the carport. I reached for the handle on the gate, and then I looked up. It was a bright and sunny day, a good sign. I thanked the Lord for the trouble. They say, sometimes, trouble is good.

Lest We Forget

Part I
June 2000, Philadelphia, Pennslyvania

I PACKED UP ALL I would need for the two-week stay. I had taken care of my essentials: holding my mail, getting help for the garden, getting my required shots, making sure my passport was in order. I was a little anxious about this trip to the motherland. After all, being picked by lottery to take a trip of a lifetime was a blessing. Especially since predominantly Black, Imani Charter High School was picking up the bulk of the cost. The ten high schoolers who were also picked to go would experience something most young people only dreamed of. Where I grew up, folks barely talked about Africa, let alone discuss taking a trip there. These young people today have no idea what grasping a sense of culture is about. This I know to be true because at twenty-eight years old, I, Vera Jenkins, am about to really find out. Thought about culture some as a youngster, particularly when learning to play the violin. My instructor, Mrs. Colbert would often say, "Get some culture; play an instrument." Now as a teacher, I could't wait to see Africa and the culture from which Black people developed front and center.

Growing up Black in inner city Philadelphia in the 1970s was tough. As kids, we saw, we discovered later, a narrative of segregation, dishonor, violence, love, struggle and survival. Books. Yeah, that was what kept me focused, out of harm's way. The thing was in the books I read, if Black people were included, it seemed we were objects, rather than subjects of the discussion. We stood on the outside, looking in like we did not really fit. That was even when the story was about Blacks. Someone else uninformed on the reality of Black life was doing the telling, and I had to search for books both hard and long to find some semblance of recognition of what living while Black was really about.

The advent of popular films with Black people in central roles helped. It had finally seemed possible to get a more straightforward view from some texts. I was never sure why these concerns dominated my thoughts, only knew they kept me seeking a familiar kind of satisfaction, or respect with each new textual encounter. It might have had something to do with overhearing older folks' talk about not seeing enough positive Black characters anywhere.

My parents, Irma and Vernon Jenkins, were both hard working individuals. They grew up in inner city Philadelphia in the '40s and '50s when they'd gathered around the radio for entertainment. Television was a luxury that few in their neighborhoods were afforded. And when there was an occasion for television, if an African American did happen to be cast, that was such a phenomenon, they busied themselves calling everyone on the phone to announce it.

There was mostly talk about not seeing us in film. But seeing Black folks in any text struck me as important. My acquaintance, with literature and film created with African Americans in any role of substance, although somewhat daunting, piqued my curiosity. I became enamored with colored folks' matters, or the subjects where they mattered or counted enough any way to be included. The interest was first gained through reading. As a child, as fast as my mother brought home comics and other books, the faster I read them. I may have related to words, but I always wanted more from the images depicted. It was like I kept trying without success to find myself in them. Or at least catch the voices of those familiar to me.

As a Black girl, I was concerned about images. Didn't know a thing about what being Afrocentric meant. Years later, as an African American woman, I was able to put a name to something I had known naturally. For sure, the texts I had encountered, for the most part, were not Afrocentric. They did not stem from an African cultural view even if the characters were Black. They may have been about Black people, but were told by others outside of that culture. That's why, I discovered later, it seemed I was look-ing in on a story, not truly participating. More reading helped with that. I had some exposure to African culture through texts I'd read in college, and I had developed a desire to go to Africa and examine the culture up close. The practice of Kwanzaa had been happening for nearly three decades, but it wasn't until I was in my twenties, that I became familiar with Afrocentric ideas.

I talked about the concept of *Sankofa* in a conversation with my parents after I viewed the film by the same name. My mother said, "Not interested. What is there about the dark continent you need to know?"

I said, "The culture. We need to get to know the culture." My father was a little more encouraging about the idea of seeing African culture up close.

"That's fabulous Vera. Reading about the culture and seeing it are two different things. I will have to see if I can get a copy of *Sankofa* from the library. Don't think this old man will get to travel to the African continent in my lifetime," he said.

Sankofa is based on a mythical bird that twist its head toward its back, and it means go back and take. It represents a principle that progress is based on the right use of positive contributions of the past. Working as an English teacher, I wanted progress; at least more progress for young people, who I watched struggle daily. I wanted for young people what I did not get in school: a chance to examine African themes. A chance to see if knowing more about Black culture than what had been taught in the past, would help them achieve the personal and academic growth they desired. Seeing the film had helped me. It could help them, too, to recognize there were connections between Black American culture and West African culture. It had been said that the majority of our African American ancestors came from West Africa. So when the opportunity to travel there came about, I grabbed it.

After flying for what added up to about twenty hours, considering the time zones, the plane landed. I looked over at Jabali, who sat in the seat next to me, and asked, "What's going on? Where are we?"

Jabali was a thin caring guy who taught math and wore dashikis most of the time. He wore one now with a kufi also. He was reclined, eyes closed. Turning to me he said, "We're almost there. In Monrovia, Liberia now, but we'll stay on the plane. How you feel?"

"Fine," I said.

It was the first time in twelve years that aircraft had landed in Liberia and there was a layover while the press and dignitaries interacted. This was due to unrest in that region. In my window seat I saw a live band, a banner welcoming Ghana Airways, and several ladies dressed in African attire. Men in fatigues armed with semi-automatic rifles sloped down in the tall background weeds that surrounded the Roberts International Airport.

The huge aircraft consisted of three sections of seats and two aisles. Seating in the outer sections had three seats to each row, and the inner row held five. Those in my group were seated mostly in the rows on the left side of the plane although some sat in the middle section. There were about twenty academicians, ten community members and ten students all interested in the development of schools that instructed students using African themes.

The Ghana Airways flight 1263 resumed its flight for the final destination. An hour later, we reached Ghana on the western coast of Africa. It was nothing like I had imagined. I expected a denser environment with lots of bush. What I saw looked similar to other airports where I had landed. The surrounding city, I had imagined, would be more rural, less urban. Our group touched down in Accra, the capital of Ghana, in late June 2000 at 4:35 PM, Africa time.

Inside the aircraft, folks moved about, gathering up belongings, preparing to disembark. Brother Jabali stood; he put the materials he had been reading inside of his backpack that was in front of him on his seat. Ms. Crystal, a science teacher, who had sat next to Brother Jabali, was in the aisle reaching up top to retrieve the things she had stored there.

Wearing white jeans and a blouse, white tennis shoes and a tan straw hat, I finally disembarked at the Kia Airport in Accra, Ghana, West Africa. When my feet left the last step of the portable staircase, I said a silent prayer of gratitude for a safe journey.

Buses went to and from various places; skycaps operated beside, under, and in front of many planes that had landed and those preparing for take-off. We were shuttled to buses that waited to transport us in groups of three. Chosen earlier, each group was bound for: The Kristoff Guesthouse in the village, the Homex Lodge or the Euro Hotel. On the bus, I sat next to my chosen roommate, Jasheri. Also an English teacher, she and I grew close over the last school year.

The first stop was the Euro Hotel. Fifteen travelers got off the bus, waving to those who had chosen other lodging. Then it was on to the Homex Lodge where another dozen or so travelers got off the bus. The last stop of the day, though by this time it was dusk, was my choice: the Kristoff Guesthouse in the Kumasi area at which the remaining dozen or so travelers got off the bus.

The massive two-story house and the grounds, which included several cars enclosed by cemented walls, had a wrought iron gated entrance. The seven foot high walls were manned by an armed sentry. The house, we were told, contained more than twenty guest rooms. The group leader, Dr. Fulton, ushered us off the bus and past the sentry at the gate. She said, "Get settled with your partner and get prepared for dinner at 9:00 PM in the main room. All are assigned an assistant who will show you to your room. Have yourselves a wonderful stay."

Jasheri and I were led to a double on the first level. She was interested in opening a charter school named for a prominent African. Her long blond locs framed a small brown face with deep-set bright brown eyes and she wore all white also except she didn't have on a hat, but an African print head wrap.

She took the bed closest to the door and I took the one by the window. The room looked similar to a typical hotel room in America, except the beds were twin with platform bottoms. Bright colored carpet covered the floor and most of the décor was red. There were two dressers and night stands and the beds had bright multicolored print throws. There was no television, but a small clock sat on one of the night stands. The view from the window was the south side of the guesthouse and a huge cement wall separating what must have been an adjacent dwelling.

"We must stick together at all times while we are here," I said.

"Yes, keep your passport on you and let me know where you are going beforehand. Are you hungry? Because I am starved!"

"I could eat."

We sat on our beds, legs crossed. On that first evening in the motherland, Jasheri and I talked, unpacked and relaxed until dinner.

At dinner, held in the big dining room, we gathered around a long table set in front of a large picture window; the view included the front of the guesthouse, several cars in the driveway, and the guarded entrance to the complex structure. There were large dishes of rice, different kinds, some with fish, some with beans and rice with chicken. The guests were served drinks without ice, condiments of spicy sauce made with palm oil and melon fruits. The rice dishes were served buffet style. There were fifteen or more people in the room with paintings on the wall and a music box in the corner. The drinks and condiments were set by two young people who appeared to be about sixteen years old. Dr. Fulton referred to them and announced, "These two will provide guesthouse services for the entire group during your stay." I grabbed Jasheri's hand who sat next to me as we bent our heads in prayer.

As we listened to soft music and ate, I said to Brother Jabali who sat on my right, "I am not accustomed to eating so much rice at one meal and I need ice in my drinks, especially in the summertime. Look at the fruit. Not sure I can eat that."

Jabali looked over at the side bar where shriveled melons were arranged. "I think I will skip that too, but the rice dishes are very good."

Except for the guarded entranceway, the guesthouse looked a lot like some structures in Philadelphia. Despite misconceptions about the backwardness of Africa, there was a large television in the front room for entertainment and an up-to-date sound and computer system. After dinner, a few guests sat in the front room and talked; one or two had cocktails and the helpers joined those in the front room for discussion on the scheduled activities for the next few days.

I sat with Jasheri on the couch, and after twenty minutes, I stood and yawned.

"You going to the room now?" she asked.

"Yes, you coming? We need to rise early so I'm going to retire now."

The plan was to get up early the following day, have breakfast and get on the bus to pick up the other two groups for a tour of El Mina Castle, a slave holding site. A few important details either were left out or I did not hear them because in the morning there were a few surprises that made me one of the last to board the departing bus.

Day Two

AFTER HER SHOWER, JASHERI came into our room, turban on her head, carrying toiletries. She said, "Be quick about it Vera, so we can eat and get on the bus." She proceeded to give directions. "Go left out this door. There is one room on the left with a sink for oral care; then the door in the middle down the hall closes on the commode. The door on the right is where you shower."

"Three doors?" What about the other door at the end of the hallway?

"It's locked, and oh, the water is cold," she said. I'd hoped what I heard her say was not right since I wanted and needed a hot shower.

When I entered the shower room, got undressed and stepped in the stall, I found it hard to use the cold water shower.

Jasheri knocked on the door. "What are you doing? We need to move it."

"I can't do my kitty-kat with this cold water."

"Just be quick. You get used to it after ten seconds down there."

I thought, *After ten seconds, shoot, I don't think I can stand one second.*

"How do you get used to a chill like that down there?" I asked through the door.

"Take my word; it's not as hard as you think, and we've got to go Vera."

She was right. I closed my eyes, gripped the handheld shower head in my right hand, and lowered it while holding onto the wall with my left. In one swift upward motion, the cold spray shot between my thighs. "Whew" escaped my lips. It was biting, like diving or jumping in a cold ocean or swimming pool. The initial shock of the cold water was the worst part. As I exited the shower room, I saw the female helper coming toward me.

I nodded and she smiled. "Pel." She said her name. I had already introduced myself. She was very dark skinned, wore braids, had a petite build and she had on white cotton shorts, a straw hat, and a light colored cotton blouse. The primary attendant for me and Jasheri, Pel had a quiet spirit, was very attentive, seemed good natured, and efficiently managed the laundry and menu orders we gave to her.

As Jasheri and I boarded the idling bus, all eyes were on us. "Good morning," we said in unison and received a few low greetings. Some were reading, some looking out the windows, and some just kept their eyes downward. Dr. Fulton was bent forward in the front seat talking with the driver. We were the final passengers to get on, and the bus lurched forward. We sat midway in the bus. Jasheri looked over at me from the window seat.

"What's the matter?" I asked.

"Did you see the look on Dr. Fulton's face when we got on the bus late?"

"No, I was making sure I had my sunglasses and hat. Don't worry about her. She'll be okay."

"Uh huh. You know we got a tight schedule. How was the shower?" She was smiling when she asked this.

"Cold."

On the way to El Mina, and after picking up the other groups, the bus had a flat tire. On the side of the road, some of the travelers stood while the driver fixed the flat. He was a middle-aged man with a navy uniform, including a cap. Off to the side of the road was a lean-to and three of us ventured over to relieve ourselves. The door to the privy was half on its hinge and inside there were millions of flies; the stench was overpowering, but the facility itself was the challenge. In the middle of the dirt floor was a hole with a two-by-four wooden board cover. With good reason, we had to finish our business quickly as the combination of heat and odor was overwhelming. Ruth, who appeared to be much older than the rest of us, seemed more adept at using a lean-to than the others.

Ruth was the spouse of Reverend Pryor. Like her husband, she was short, but unlike him, she was stout. Ruth was quiet, wore her salt and pepper hair pulled back in a bun, and she wore a wide brim hat, sandals and loose fitting cotton clothing and sunglasses. She had an affable air, and was light skinned with a round freckled face. She straddled the hole in the earth, relieved herself and stepped out in a matter of what seemed like one minute. Her husband was over by the bus and he kept his eye on the make-shift potty. When we were all done, we joined the others.

Reverend Pryor had black shiny hair that was smoothed down flat and curled at the nape. He wore prescription glasses, stood about five-foot-two and weighed roughly one hundred sixty pounds. Reverend Pryor, with medium brown skin, had a soothing voice, sort of a V-shaped face and small lips. Although he wore casual clothes, including sandals and a cotton shirt and slacks, he exuded an air of authority.

Back on the road, there was little conversation. The privy experience and the heat combined was enough for me to preserve my energy and be still.

Being still was apparently not something the Ghanaian children were accustomed to as they swarmed the group when we emerged from the castle. The castle experience had also been very emotional; folks were crying as they exited. We were told by the guide that enslaved Africans were sent on the middle passage from El Mina. I caught a glimpse of Psalm 133 written overtop the entranceway to the castle. *"How good and pleasant it is when God's people live together in unity."* It seemed to indicate 'all is well within these walls.' *Au contraire*, I thought.

Inside the castle, we observed slave trade artifacts like shackles, and iron head gear with metal plungers. The head gear, we were told, were used to force feed the enslaved that refused to eat. The plunger thingy bashed out teeth in the most brutal way. There were faded images on the walls of personal items for enslaved Africans like rough ragged clothing, and troughs that they ate from like animals. There were make-shift slave pens. A built in fortress was up top with cannons to protect the slaver's human goods from invaders. All of this in the midst of biblical passages over the top of doors, in the hallways, and all over the walls in the various rooms. It was dank inside and smelled like a damp cellar. There was another smell I couldn't quite identify, but there was nothing pleasant about it.

As we were led outside, most in the group were quiet, somber, and looked down. We seemed to be moving in slow motion. But the children ran around the group nodding toward their opened hands. Back on the bus, the group quietly passed a collection plate that was actually a plastic bag and gave this to the children who swarmed the bus. I found it difficult to speak, the castle experience was so sad; I just stared out the window at the birds pecking the sidewalk for crumbs. It was heartbreaking to know that humans who looked like me were held, beaten, treated like animals, and traded all in the name of legal lifetime bondage, called slavery. What kind of people does that to another?

After El Mina, the groups stopped for dinner by the beach. There we had a marvelous meal of fried fish, including grilled crawfish, soup, roasted root vegetables, sauce and fruit. The open air, the drumming that accompanied meals, the beach, and the delicious food provided a relaxed atmosphere. Later that evening on the way back to the hotels, the bus had another flat. Waiting on the side of the road while the driver fixed the flat was creepy for me. It was dark and deserted. We waited for over an hour, arriving at the guesthouse after midnight.

On subsequent days, the groups toured the downtown Kamasi area, including the cultural center where literature, gifts and wares of the natives were available. Day trips included the bank to exchange American money for the currency accepted in Ghana called cides. Most evenings were spent sitting on the grounds of the guesthouse listening to music, and talking.

Day four of the trip included experiencing a Homowah in the center of Accra during the hottest part of the day: one o'clock. We visited with the chief of the Ga people, had libation with hot gin that we drank from the common cup. The Homowah was a ceremonial gathering where red clothing was worn by invitees, and included a parade of African dance, drumming and gunfire in recognition of the village elders, the chief and key Ga people. Key people were those who made great sacrifices, including feeding others who were unable to provide for themselves. The Ga people lived in poor conditions; their homes were without indoor plumbing, and there was a scarcity of food and other necessities including toilet paper.

After a traditional meal of fish, soup and cornmeal, the group took pictures and was offered a corn drink, a warm substance resembling tea; it was bitter.

I whispered to Jasheri, "I'm gonna have to find a bathroom."

Jasheri said, "Ask that attendant over there where you can go." She pointed in the direction of a young person standing away from the guests, her hands clasped in front of her.

"Excuse me," I said to this young person who had served the drinks. "I need to use the facility."

The girl, who appeared to be about sixteen, directed me to an older woman of about eighty who motioned with her curled pointer finger for me to follow her. She was a little more than four feet tall, bent over, and the color of pumpernickel bread. The skin on her hands and arms resembled the outside of a raisin, and she looked at me from deep set dark eyes.

Outside the building where the group had eaten, and around the side, down a small path, the old woman led me to what looked like a hut; it had a dirt floor, one tiny room that was crammed with all kinds of things including a bicycle that hung from the rear wall, a cooking space, and books stacked on the floor and on a small table. It also had what looked like a mat for sleeping.

The old woman's only spoken word was "Come." She handed me a bowl and nodded toward a corner in the room. I looked at the bowl, which could hold about ten ounces, and reached in my purse for a tissue. I then lifted my red skirt, and right there in the hut, I relieved myself. When the woman nodded at the bowl that I had filled, I handed it to her and returned the way I had come.

Guests stood around mingling with the natives; a speaker was on a makeshift podium discussing the Homowah. I eased through the folks and beside Jasheri. She asked, "How'd you make out?"

"I'll have to tell you all about it, but I went in a bowl in a little place in the back."

"You went in a bowl? Where is the bowl?"

"I gave it to the old woman."

"What old woman? Chile, what did she do with the contents of the bowl, throw it out the door?"

"I don't know; since they don't waste anything here, I suppose she found use for it."

"Girl, we gotta watch the amount of water we drink here. Don't want nobody carrying off my liquid. Can't say where it might end up."

"You do have a point. Think we can get a ride with Brother Hampton back to the guesthouse since he's going back early to pick up something? I heard him say that and I'm hot out here."

"I'ma ask him."

"Let's go; he's right over there," I said.

We walked over yonder to speak with Brother Hampton and as we did, we passed a young child about six years old sitting on a rock handling cow feet; cow feet is used for seasoning greens. The child, wrapped in a ragged cloth, hair uncombed, had no shoes. In her hands she held what looked like a scouring pad, and she rubbed the blackness off of the bottom of the cow foot, and then placed it in a bowl or calabash. The hooves in the calabash did not look as if much of the blackness had been removed, but the little one continued with this process while she sat in the open hot sun.

On one of the final days of our tour, the group visited Wesley Methodist Church where Reverend Pryor was invited to speak; this was a grand edifice with stained glass windows, multiple pews and elaborate furnishings. In the front of the church appeared a vast pulpit with more than twenty-five velvet upholstered chairs. It was communion Sunday and the choirs were outstanding. They sang very well and looked very good. One choir wore gradua-tion caps, and the other had robes of white silk with matching head coverings. Our group sat on the left side of the pulpit and a Ghanaian translated Reverend Pryor's sermon titled: "When the Going is Rough." The service was four hours long.

After church, the group was invited to the home of a village dignitary for lunch of fish soup and rice, plantain, cabbage and pineapple juice. After prayer and supplication, we boarded our bus that took us back to our respective lodging places. At the Kristoff Guesthouse, we danced until 12:30 AM, then retired for the night.

The last day of the tour was spent shopping, sightseeing and visiting a weaving village that, in addition to fabrics, sold Ashanti gold. It was early afternoon, and the bus took us to the village via a very steep winding road. As the bus made its way up the hill, I thought it might tilt backward because of the way it groaned and jerked. The bus was also not in the best of shape.

The seats were worn, the tires looked smooth, and it did not have air conditioning.

On the left hand side of the road, I noticed what looked like huge dirt piles. I pointed to the dirt piles that stood five feet tall with little poke holes on the side and at the top. I asked the tour guide, a young thin male with bright dark eyes that had a yellow tint, "What are those?"

He said, "Those are ant hills." Then he roared back with laughter. I thought, *If those are ant hills, the size of the ants must be humongous.* I made a mental note not to get anywhere near them. One of the things also discovered was that due to the prevalence of malaria, a condition developed from the water in these regions, many Africans had yellow tint in their eyes. Other than the tint in his eye, the tour guide appeared quite healthy, especially if one judged from his bright white set of teeth.

The bus pulled under a makeshift awning attached to a small dwelling and the group disembarked. Many individuals explored the various places in the village from weaving shops, fabric stores, and jewelry and wood shops. The area looked like an open strip from Western times with shops on either side of the road. The strip was about four hundred yards long and the width was that of a wide street back home in the hood. I explored the jewelry and found earrings made with cut glass, a twenty-four karat gold Sankofa pennant for my gold neck chain, and I purchased bulk orange and green kente cloth. Then I sat and watched the loom operator.

The loom took up a large part of the shop. It was an intricate sewing machine-like construction with an old fashioned rock pedal underneath. At its side were several pelts of fabric. The loom had long wooden thin slats protruding from it that weaved in and out of each other to produce the pelts and cloth patterns.

The loom operator was a very dark skinned, thin, aging old man who spoke little English. While he hummed a soft tune, he moved methodically on the machine back and forth; although his arms and body seemed small, he had a very wide reach as he moved his arms in and out and between the slats. His feet were in constant movement back and forth spurring the machine along. And then he stopped and smiled at me and the other two travelers, one of which was Jasheri who had wandered into the shop. He spread his hands in the direction of the bright colored fabric and then he went back to his work. In the tiny shop, while he worked, he sat on a small wooden stool that looked as if it could barely support one hundred pounds. Clearly the old man had a work ethic that evidently went a long way back. He was focused, methodical and not at all distracted by the travelers. He went about his work in a determined and practiced fashion.

Near sunset, the group boarded the bus. The view on the hilltop was encased in a magnificent orange glow from the sun. Then children appeared from everywhere, out of the little shops, from around corners, from the nearby fields, and they began to rock the bus. This frightened me and the rest of the travelers appeared alarmed; so did the tour guide and the driver. There were many "oohs." Some "ahhs." Still some hollered out, "Hold on."

The barefoot children spoke in their native language, but I did not understand. What I thought, apparently along with some of the others, was the children wanted something from the bus-load of travelers. Again, a collection was taken among the group members while the bus rocked back and forth with the force of many hands. The collection was given to the tallest, lankiest young person near the door.

In his own language, the young boy said something to the other children that made them stop. There was a huge sigh of relief, and the bus moved on down the windy hill while the sun fully set. It was a fruitful and, at the same time, scary experience. With one hand placed over my heart, my breathing began a more even rhythm. Although a bit frightened, I had a satisfying feeling overall. It was part relief and part regret that my Ghana excursion would soon end. Similar to how the last pages of a memorable book signals the end. Wanting and, at the same time, not wanting it to be over.

Visiting the weaving village left a lasting impression. Weaving cloth is a significant part of African culture. I would always remember that African people were no strangers to hard work. That was imprinted in my mind. I saw how hard the weavers worked; and I knew while enslaved, Black folks worked from can't see in the morning to can't see at night. I could sense that the folks in that weaving village toiled each day to scratch out a living. I knew it was hard work.

Back at the hotel, I shared my thoughts with Jasheri. She sat on her bed, open empty suitcase beside her. Brother Jabali knocked on the door.

"Come in," she said.

"What's going on?" he asked.

"Nothing," I said. "Have a seat." I moved from the middle of my bed where I'd sat cross-legged, toward the edge. Patting the hard mattress' edge close to the head of the bed, I invited him to sit. Jasheri exhaled.

She said, "Vera was talking about her impressions of the slave castles we visited. She said she would tell her students how we must continue the struggle. Tell them how our people have been scrapping by, surviving for their benefit."

"Yeah," Jabali said. "I will put a human face on the struggle to survive by teaching them about the genius of the African. The ability to survive what must have been desperation. Maybe help them come up with solutions to desperation in their home communities."

I continued, "My parents told me that scraping to get by was what we had always done. Nothing new. As a child, I just didn't know it. But, I will never forget that when we arrived, the fight had to seem impossible. We must have fought hard to fit in what had to feel like a foreign culture. We're still fighting. To feel like valued participants in American culture. That's hard work. *We* all learned this firsthand from the education industry; it was and still is hard work for African Americans. We had to be two times as equipped to do the job as another. Hard work."

"Uh huh," Brother Jabali and Jasheri said calmly.

I said, "A brother in the school system that I liked, once said to me, 'Come, join the wild side of life, teach.' He knew teaching was rough. When I began teaching, it was tough. So, I tried to stimulate students using stories. I did this. Still do. I was led to tell a young person that to make progress, they must imagine riding a bicycle with two hundred extra pounds in tow. 'That's hard,' they had said."

"Hard, yes," I said. "But it may inspire struggling students like you, without proper resources to fight harder to achieve. Maybe help balance things. When I told them that to make any headway, they may have to walk away from a small injustice to preserve energy for the bigger ones coming, that was hard for me. It was right to tell them that walking away now, may give them another day to do something greater. But I had hope that the burden of telling them to defer their desires was greater for me than for them; that ultimately it would lead to victory. That they could be triumphant despite the arrogance of privileged students who had the means to succeed. We know that takes a lot of convincing, a lot of motivating. Hard work."

"Uh huh," Jasheri said. "When we set out to help students honor cultural realities of suffering, we knew it wasn't gonna be easy. And if what the elders say about hard work rings true, in rememberance, let it be instructive: What don't kill you will make you stronger."

I looked over at Jabali and then to Jasheri as we sat nodding in agreement. Jasheri reached her left hand out and I took it in my right; with my left hand, I reached for Jabali's. We sat in a circle for a minute, heads bowed, eyes closed. I said a prayer for the hard work, the struggle, that it not be in vain.

"Amen," we said in unison.

Part II
June 2004 – Philadelphia, Pennsylvania

ON MY THIRTY-SECOND BIRTHDAY, I received notice my proposal to participate in the university international program in West Africa was granted. I had taught in the English department for the past three years. On a humbug, I thought it worth submitting an application to the yearly offerings to travel abroad. I wanted to return to West Africa, but thought the cost and commitment was out of my reach. I mentioned to my office-mate, Gretchen, my interest in submitting a persuasive text that would get the granting committee's attention. "Go for it," was what she'd said.

Gretchen and I taught courses in the same department part time while she pursued graduate studies. I worked as an administrator for a charater schools' consortium in Pennsylvania. Anxious about my proposal, I said to her, "Wouldn't it be ironic if the university sponsored my return to West Africa?" We sat in our usual spots at our desks that were butted up against each other's, staring into our computer screens. I looked up into her soft eyes as she smiled at me. I thought that a positive sign as I hit the send button on my email.

When I read the reply email to my proposal that early June morning granting me full support, it had been exactly four years since my first trip to the region. "Your proposal to travel to West Africa in July 2004 has been granted. You must respond immediately to confirm and be aware that due to the competitive nature of the application process and the level of planning required to solidify program plans with the host sites, the university frowns upon applicants who cancel."

We traveled by van service on an early Friday morning in July from my home in Philadelphia with three other professionals on our way to John F. Kennedy Airport in New York City. I glanced out of the window at the scenery. The fifteen-passenger van made its way over the Pennsylvania Turnpike, headed east toward the Holland Tunnel. Tall grass blanketed both sides of the road where single homes sat back off the highway. Not much of a view except I noticed some of the homes had elaborate wooden decks in the rear with intricately placed stairs that sloped on a weird angle from the house to the ground below. I'd had an interesting conversation with the gentleman who was in the van when the driver picked me up.

Sidney was an artist on his way to catch a flight to Paris. He talked about his previous use of the limousine service on his many trips around the world. Sidney said that he planned to visit the motherland on future trips after he found out my destination. He was a small man who wore dark rimmed glasses; his tan complexion and medium length brown hair complimented his indulgent eyes and cheerful smile. Sidney made small talk about his artwork as the van weaved through the traffic making excellent time for my 12:30 PM flight.

Blessed was how I felt about my opportunity to go back to West Africa, only this time my destination was Senegal. The icing on the cake was that the university was footing the bill.

Comfortable with the reading material I had chosen for the long trip and the arrangements made for my cat Silver, I had locked up my house and prayed for traveling mercies for the long journey.

At John F. Kennedy Airport, I handed the university credit card to the van driver for the first half of the trip, and confirmed my anticipated returned date. The driver handed me a receipt. "So long and safe journey," I said to the others.

The driver said, "Miss, you need help with your bags?"

"Thank you." I tipped him and made my way through the automatic door.

I checked in at the counter for the first leg of my journey that included a stop in Chicago. It was only 9:30 AM. I took the escalator to the gate area and glanced around for a place to eat. I slung my carry-on up on my shoulder and found a seat in the food court.

After settling on a seat by the railing where travelers walked to and fro, I took out my mystery novel and read a few pages. Then I went up to the counter and ordered my breakfast that included crepes, fruit and yogurt. I ate and glanced around at the travelers in the brightly lit food court. Finally, it was time to make my way toward the gate. I found another forty to fifty people waiting in the gate area where I took a seat. My flight was called, and with passport and plane ticket in hand, I boarded the aircraft. On board the jet, I located my assigned window seat, excused myself and climbed over the man in the aisle seat. I took out my cell and called my mother.

"Good morning, Mom. I'm *on* board." I dragged out the last two words.

"You're kidding. You're using your cell?"

"Yes. When we take off, I must turn it off."

"It's cloudy here."

"I see a few clouds 'cause I'm in the window seat."

Suddenly, the sky lit up with a flash of lightning and a sudden downpour engulfed the plane. I looked out the window while the rain pounded in a steady stream; the rain droned on the roof and big droplets ran down to the sill. *If this don't stop we could be delayed.*

"What was that?"

"That is rain. It's pouring now. Ain't that something? Call you when I get there. Love you."

"Make sure you do. Have a safe trip."

The pilot said over the PA system, the flight would be delayed until the rain subsided. I read my book while a baby two rows behind started crying. The crying went on and on and the flight attendant served drinks and snacks while the plane sat on the runway. One hour passed and the rain continued; two hours led to three and the storm did not let up. After five and one half hours on the runway with a crying baby on board flight 725, the pilot finally announced, "Prepare for takeoff."

Seven hours later, I landed in Brussels long after I should have arrived. Since I had missed my connecting flight, I was directed by the attendant to the airline counter to manage another. Disappointment began to take hold, but was short lived.

The counter attendant in her airline gear including a crisp shirt and bow tie, greeted me with a smile. She was a blonde of average height with a professional air. She said, "Good evening Ms. Jenkins. It looks like we must put you on a flight to Madrid and from there you will connect with your flight to Senegal. You are in luck, as we do not have any more coach seats on that connecting flight and therefore you will fly to Senegal business class. Enjoy your flight. You will be boarding your Madrid flight at gate six in about twenty minutes."

I had never flown business class, and was anxious to reach my final destination. Tired from the long delay, and somewhat discombobulated from all the shifting around, I laid my head back and anticipated the last leg of my long journey.

In Madrid, I made a smooth connection to my final flight. Again, I was enthusiastically greeted by the flight attendant and I took my seat in the business section of the huge aircraft. There were four rows of seats, two on both sides of the short aisle, which ended at a quarter moon shaped bar. There was one man in the window seat of the row where I sat. The attendant helped me remove my jacket, smiled and presented me with three different newspapers including the *Times*. She said, "What can I get you to drink?"

"Bourbon, please," I said, thinking that would relax me. I read the newspapers while the man next to me struck up a conversation.

Habib was Senegalese, returning home from a Software Company business trip; he was young, white, about thirty-five years old. His olive skin, straight black hair and thick build, complimented bright dark eyes. He seemed sincere when he told me about the places I should make sure to see while in Senegal.

He even offered touring services to the local museum if needed; said he and his wife would be available to take me, and he gave me his card.

"Thank you."

When I tried unsuccessfully to reach my assigned tour guide by phone, Habib glanced over at my pad. He explained that the number of digits I had contained less numbers than required to reach a party in Senegal.

"I can assist you with getting a shuttle to the hotel." Habib said that his wife would pick him up at the airport and that I could ride with them. "There, look." He pointed out the window at the coastline of Senegal that came into view.

An announcement from the pilot said the plane was approaching Senegal and would land in a few minutes.

The bourbon had relaxed me and I confidently disembarked with Habib following, strode into the airport and waited by the carousel to claim my bags. A few security personnel were observed in the unexpectedly small area. It seemed easy to spot the tourist from the natives milling about, and there were about one hundred people in all including airport personnel. There were two customs counters for all travelers that had to be processed.

I observed Habib passionately greet a slim blond woman with a ponytail. She eagerly returned the greeting and spoke to him in French. Then they joined me at the carousel to claim luggage. Habib's processing took much longer than mine and during the wait, I chatted with the young blonde who had been introduced as his wife. Rebecca was knowledgeable about Senegalese culture. She spoke fluent English and switched back and forth between both languages.

When Habib joined us, it was somewhat easy to follow what they were saying to each other in French since their body language spoke volumes. Appearng very eager to be reunited, after being apart for the last month, their hands explored each other's bodies as they embraced.

The Mrs. wrote down a few sights and her phone number on a piece of paper. She offered to take me sightseeing later in the week if my tour guide did not show me the significant Senegal sites that she had indicated on the note with her phone number. Rebecca concurred with her husband that my contact number for the Novotel Hotel was missing a digit, and she offered to drive me there since it was en route to their residence. She said, "If you do not mind, we must stop for water." After considering several factors like, the sincerity of the couple, the way they interacted with the airport authorities—-several airport employees had greeted Habib by his first name including the security personnel, and the fact that they shared their identification and business card information, I agreed.

"I really appreciate your help with a ride and I may call you during my stay," I said.

Together we walked toward the airport exit and located their Jeep Cherokee. "Let me put your bags in the back," Habib said.

"Thanks." I climbed up in the back and Rebecca rode up front with her husband. It was close to 9:00 PM. We took the river drive toward the Novotel, stopped at a convenience store, and then we were en route again. Rebecca chatted away about how she missed Habib, and I looked out the passenger window at the moonlit rolling waters that seemed to spread outward for miles.

Twenty hours after my departure from Philadelphia, I was driven five more miles in fifteen minutes toward the hotel. On the way, we had a view of the Atlantic Ocean the entire trip. Rebecca pointed out several sites that she had recommended earlier, and the Jeep approached the unlit hotel. My brow furrowed and Rebecca explained the darkness.

Observing the circular driveway, where several individuals mulled about, Rebecca said, "There has apparently been a blackout." She said that blackouts had occurred during the past week, but they generally only lasted a few moments. Habib pulled up to the dark structure and helped with bags. He reminded me to call if I needed an escort during my stay. "Akwabaa," they both said in unison as I headed up to the front door. This I soon discovered meant, 'Welcome.'

In the dim lobby, several individuals carried drinks. Some were talking to each other and some were just hanging out. At the desk, the blackout was confirmed by the receptionist who told me to please wait a few minutes until the problem was resolved. She said the keys to the rooms would not work without electricity. The tiny lights came from a few candles placed on tables.

I found the bar to my left; on my right were two elevators and to their right hung a huge framed portrait. I found a stool and ordered bottled water. The man sitting on the stool next to me said good evening, and it turned out that he was Chadd who had traveled from Tennessee to meet with the same group that I would. He said he taught history at the university. After I drank half of my water, the lights came on. Cheers went up and my reservation was processed.

Since I had a scheduled meeting in the conference room of the hotel with the rest of the group in the morning, and I was anxious to check in, I waved at Chadd and said, "See you tomorrow." An attendant escorted me from the elevator to my room on the second floor. Once there, I tipped him and locked the door. I sat on the bed, only after I first checked underneath. There was nothing out of the ordinary there. I drank the rest of my bottled water, and retired for the night.

Early the next morning, two days after leaving Philadelphia, I awoke rested and opened the heavy drapes at the window. Outside of my window, I saw the ocean less than one hundred yards away. The view was breathtaking, and I felt the long trip was worth it just for the view I would have for two weeks. The furnishings included two double beds, a dresser table and chair, a television that sat on top of the chest of drawers, a few sparse paintings and a wall length glass view of the ocean that opened onto a small balcony.

This room would certainly do, I thought as I showered and dressed in preparation for my breakfast meeting downstairs. When I arrived at the conference room to continental breakfast, several individuals were observed seated in a circle including the tour guide. Serigne Ndiaye, a deeply pigmented thin man, had a white toothy grin and wire rimmed eyeglasses. "*Akwabaa*," he said.

"Thank you." After helping myself to breakfast, I glanced around the room. In the brightly lit conference style setting I counted eight participants, not including the tour guide who would spend the next two weeks together in a seminar on the historical and cultural developments in Senegal. Right away my eyes settled on two other African American females. The others, except for Serigne, were white.

After introductions, the schedule was reviewed; we would stay at the Novotel for the next six nights after which the plan included a three night stay at a local fishing village and then our return to the Novotel Hotel for the remainder of the seminar.

The rest of the day was slated for rest and relaxation. That evening, four of us, Chadd, Kris, David and I walked to dinner to the Keur N'Deye at 68 Rue Vincens about ten blocks from the Novotel. We ate grilled food and Senegalese dishes including fish and rice, and Chebujan, a chicken with smothered onions and gravy dish. For dessert we had petite French desserts. We made it back to the hotel at 11:00 PM.

The next few days included a series of lectures, visiting places like the Cheik Ante Diop University, the downtown Baobab cultural center, the President's gated palace, the Dakar Media Center, and the local market for wine and snacks. We also frequented the bank for exchange of currency.

One downtown place that served the best 'Chebujan' in town was the Almadies. We ate outdoors and watched the sun set during our meals. On the way back to the hotel, several tailors approached us offering their services including tailor made outfits and bulk cloth. We received invitations for personal fittings at various shop locations, but the most magnificent sights we had an opportunity to experience were the Pink Lake, Goree Island, and the Fishing Village.

We traveled to the Pink Lake by bus, a less than ideal mode of transportation. The bus was doorless and could hold no more than twenty passengers; it suffered a flat tire en route to the lake. While the group waited in a field for the driver to repair the tire, with the use of a tree branch, the tour guide helped himself to mangoes from a tree nearby. We ate them in the niney-nine-degree heat with the only shade coming from trees in the clearing. The succulently sweet fruit made up for the brutal heat, and about an hour later, we continued on toward our destination.

The renowned Pink Lake was a beach front set off the road behind a bank of trees. The pink color came from the sun and from the salts in the water. The story goes that there were mounds of salt underneath the lake that the sun mixes with to produce a deep and brilliant pink. We got this from the locals. A lone fisherman appeared on the water harvesting salts with a long rod type apparatus. As we watched, several natives appeared out of seemingly nowhere, one carrying a fruit basket and others peddling their various wares like beads and trinkets.

An African woman, her head and body wrapped in colorful cloth, approached Niama and me. The older woman extended one hand with the other resting on her ample hip. This give-and-take pose said she wanted to negotiate something. I had brought toiletries and lipsticks while Niama had pens, rings and ribbons. We exchanged these for handmade earrings.

On the beach we collected sea shells and salt rocks; the folks that lived there wore huge smiles and walked confidently about. Amidst extreme poverty, they seemed gracious for the attention given their humble dwelling. A lean-to here and there made up their shelter and living quarters. Our group mingled and mulled around the natives, some communicating in French.

Our outing was topped off with a meal in a nearby restaurant with a clear view of the setting sun over the lake. I could only imagine the wonders of the next site on our schedule.

Goree Island sat on the western tip of the Senegambia region. One must access it by ferry. Serigne took the group to the dock waiting area where more than fifty people waited for the ferry to the island. They were mainly women with children. Some of the women carried sacks and darted their eyes.

I had on khaki pants, sandals, and a sleeveless blouse. A large brimmed hat was pulled down tightly over my braided hair, and trinklets for exchange were stowed in my bag that was slung across my shoulder. A notepad and snacks for the day's journey were also in tow.

The ferry attendant motioned for the people to board, and out of the corner of my eye, as I boarded, a very thick African woman with three children peered over at me. I proceeded toward seats on the first level, which filled first. My group made their way on and found single seats where they could. Some climbed the short ladder to the next level; still others took seats on the bench next to where I sat with the thick woman and her children. Overcrowding resulted in people standing when the ferry left the dock. Hips and arms touched on the bench as we sat quietly on the ride over. The woman with the children pointed to my earrings and motioned with a bracelet that she wanted to swap. I smiled at her and the children, and shook my head. She then held up earrings with a coral stone. I asked, "How much?" She nodded toward my earrings. I shook my head slightly then looked out at the water.

I do not intend to part with my earrings if I can help it, although that woman looks determined to convince me otherwise. As the ferry made its way toward the island, I leaned back, while the water shimmered.

Twenty minutes later, the attendant jumped to the narrow landing, tied the ferry to a stud jutting out of the water, as the surf lapped at the sides of the vessel, and motioned with his hand for the passengers to follow him.

I hesitated at what seemed to be a huge jumping distance.

Then with an accent the attendant said, "Come, it is okay."

I hopped off as did the many other passengers to begin the one hundred-yard walk to the island. It was so bright and sunny I had to shield my eyes.

Our group tour guide on the island, an older, leathery-looking short man, directed us toward a path that wound up and around a hill for about one half mile. Single file, we walked along toward the top of the hill and looked down. At the top of the hill in the open field were cannons.

The view at the top was spectacular. The docked ferry sat idly on the vast ocean while goats grazed near a house with a yard full of cotton clothing hanging on a clothesline. Several other buildings of all shapes and colors neatly lined the area below where little children ran around playing with animals. A small group of children played on a little stretch of sandy beach. There was a post office, and a grove of trees. The trees most likely made it cooler down there than the seemingly one hundred degrees at the top of the hill.

The cannons were used to protect the island and the human cargo once held there. The Dutch and Portuguese slavers had known well the prize of Goree; it was originally referred to as "Good Raid" by slave catchers because of the abundance of enslaved Africans, then subsequently named Goree. It was situated in such a way that made it convenient from the top of the hill to detect oncoming ships. The canons were strategically placed to deter unwanted ships from docking, and the convenience for the ships at Goree was its location and proximity to a direct route to the Americas. I asked, "What is that pink-looking building down below?"

The tour guide explained. "A slave holding structure with the *door of no return*. The building is pink due to the blood of the enslaved." I shuddered. He explained further.

"Because of the history of slavery, property on Goree Island can no longer be owned by the whites." Presently it is owned by African people only and used chiefly as a tourist sight."

My group made their way down the winding path, past the post office and around another path toward the pink clay two-story ominous-looking building. Inside, as the tour guide led us, we observed severall rooms on the left and on the right. Above each entryway, a sign appeared, each one indicating its inhabitants: babies, men, women, and children. A railing wound all the way around the top floor behind which additional rooms sat, and encircled a narrow landing. Up top, we looked down on entrances to rooms and the open dirt-floor area in the middle.

At the back of the building were still more slave pens and the tour guide led us to where the lighting was poorer the further we walked away from the front door. Beyond one pen in the rear was the '*door of no return.*' On the other side of the door the vast ocean beckoned. This was where ships had docked to load the human cargo.

Another room in the back had a sign over the entrance that read "boys." There was a small window on the rear wall with vertical iron bars three inches apart. The tour guide explained that. "The enslaved young African males were held with many others and with their waste, food, disease, and anguish all together in the dank place waiting to be handed to the ship mates through that open window." He nodded toward the window wth the bar.

Waving his hands in animated fashion, he asked the group gathered around him: "What do the slave traders do with the thick Africans who cannot fit through the space between the bars?"

We looked at each other and at him blankly.

He answered his own question. "They starved them until they fit even as the enslaved male children moaned, which was oftentimes all they could do, if they did not perish from the filth and unhealthy conditions in the room."

Tears welled up in my eyes, as I sensed the spirit of the babies and the young people, including adult enslaved women and men in the pens. Like some of the other group members, I had to leave the slave house and get some air. The tour guide's booming voice continued to discuss the history of Goree. As I ventured toward the front of the building, I heard him explain, "The landing on the second floor was used by the slave catchers who stayed in the upper rooms, to peer down on enslaved females on the bottom landing. The females were brought out in the open naked for inspection; the slave catchers would then choose the one they wanted, and then the women were hosed down. They had also been held in their own waste, their menses, dirt, and whatever food scrapes they managed.

"The slave traders could do whatever they wanted with them. After the women were used and abused, they were returned to the female holding pens until they were boarded onto ships bound for the Americas."

I don't think that I could have lived through something like that. In fact, I know I couldn't.

Stunned, I sat on a bench outside the slave house. I could not speak and my stomach flipped and flopped. Two female group members sat silently nearby. I found out later, like me, they'd had similar physical and emotional reactions to the slave house experience.

Also later, from the tour guides and the literature on the

island, the group learned of the history of sordid relations between the slave traders and the women.

Africans were at the whim of the Dutch and the Portuguese men whose enslaving work, from which they became quite rich, required them to be away from home for long periods, maybe six months or more at a time. The married slave catchers created contracts with their wives that permitted them to have relations with enslaved women on Goree during these long periods. The women gathered neccessary food items by traveling through underground tunnels on the island, and at the whim of enslavers, prepared their foods.

The enslaved African women had no say in the contract. However, a group of young women called the Signares created a plan of their own. Kept out of sight, these women moved through the tunnels and often found others who spoke their language. The massive enslavement process had placed Africans from different villages, who spoke various languages, together on the island. This made communications challenging, but determination to survive forced them to find a way. The way, the Signares decided, was to somehow draw other young enslaved women into their plan.

The imbalance of having only the enslavers benefit from the primarily sexual relationship with the Signares, was offered as a worthy reason for others to buy into their plan. Their strategy included putting ground glass and plant substances in the foods they prepared; they then manipulated the minds of the men during sex. When some of the men became ill and even died, the women made their moves. Although dangerous, with sexual favors, the women broke down further the men's resistance and negotiated compensation for some of what they endured. And they achieved some bargaining room with the men. The women made the men feel better, even good, and the women got valuable jewelry, gems and money in exchange for their services. Together these savvy women amassed a fortune. According to legend, then they could buy their own and their family members' freedoms.

The rest of our time on the island we watched the young African children playing on the beach, and we had dinner at an open café. At dinner, most in the group did not eat, just moved food around on their plates, and conversation was minimal. The effects of the island and what we had discovered seemed to have quieted us. I had a beer and Chadd sat next to me, looking into his glass of tea. Niama stared into the ocean, and the tour guide announced that the ferry would soon leave the island.

I walked to the library and looked around, and found myself sitting alone on a bench thinking. I could see the beach activity below, and also several of the group members mulling about down by the café. I sat on the bench until the others moved toward the ferry. *I would probably not return to this island, but the experience will remain with me for some time. My small source of comfort was learning about the Signares. I wonder how I might have handled a situation like theirs. And I wonder why wives of the enslavers did not resist the contracts permitting their husbands to* have sex with enslaved African women; their wives may have had a fancy for other male eye candy they pretended to be afraid of, like African males, who they often accused of lusting after them.

When we returned to the hotel from Goree, I packed for the scheduled three night stay at the fishing village and emailed a few friends. Email time was set aside for early morning and after the dinner hour. It was relied upon mainly because of the difference in time zones between Senegal and the USA, but it was the most efficient option for communications while abroad.

Our mode of transportation was less efficient than I had hoped. However, the next morning, we boarded a bus with operating windows and doors that would take us to the village. The traffic was light and the bus ride was smooth; surprisingly, there were no incidences of flat tires. It was very hot out as usual and to minimize perspiration, I sat very still, even with the open windows that generated a little breeze. Three hours later, a little before noon, the bus pulled onto a narrow road with thick bush on either side. The small sign read: Taubob Fishing Village. We lurched downward as the road wound through even thicker bush. Between the narrow road and the steep decline, it seemed the bus might topple over. Finally, we drove into a clearing with several bungalows on the left that were perched high off the ground; wooden staircases led up to them.

The scenery was dreamlike. A path led to the right and stopped at a high wooden fence. We paired off and Niama and I chose a cottage on the far left at the very end.

Inside were two small rooms, including an even smaller bathroom. The room on the right had two small beds, and in the other on the left was a medium-sized bed. The bathroom was midway between the two. I went to the left and unpacked my things, then joined Niama in the larger room with the two beds. The windows were without screens, but had wooden jalousies, and there were bed nets to keep insects at bay. The toilet had a pull string on the back for flushing. There was nothing modern about the village, but it was comfortable. Woodsy and hidden like a juke joint, it was definitely not for the indoors type. I thought it a good idea to pray over the place and Niama joined me.

"Can we handle this for three nights?"

"If we pray about it, yes." Niama, like me, was spiritual. She had married a preacher. Unlike me, she was thin. She had medium brown skin and long legs on a high waist. Her mouth was prominent with large front teeth set on a small face. She seemed to have a warm spirit. We held hands as I began to pray:

"Oh, Lord, thank you for a safe journey to this village; keep us both safe while here, Lord, from all hurt, harm and danger. Bless us with good health and watch over the others in the group also; give us the power of discernment as we learn from one another, and bless us with a fruitful experience that we might teach others about the culture we are understanding. In Jesus' name we pray." I paused. "Amen."

"Amen. Now you ready to go down to the clearing?"

"Ready," I said.

In the clearing, a few group members lulled around Dr. Ndiaye waiting for the group of nine. Together, we were led up the narrow path on the right, away from the cottages and toward the high wooden fence. Before the fence, about fifty yards in, was a tiled sitting area. Foliage was on either side of what looked like drums. The cone-shaped structures were underneath a frail-looking tree with low willowy branches. Tiles were intricately placed on a low wall around the cones that held diamond shaped cut glass pieces set on blue ceramic. On the far right was a door that led to a raised eating space with a long table. Place settings and an assortment of fruits, cheeses and appetizing fish dishes sat on a side bar. In the back, was a wet bar and a gentleman taking drink orders. The room was small, yet comfortable. Two attendants directed the group's seating and answered questions about the village. The room was roofless, the sky above was clear blue, and all the while were sounds of a fiddle.

After the meal, we were led down the central path, and to the right toward the high wooden fence, Adirondack chairs were placed. To the left of the chairs, a campground-like rest room appeared. It was doorless, but open-ended partitions on stilts made up the entrance and exit. Behind the restroom was a one-story building with long silk curtains at the windows. And finally, behind the fence was the ocean with a beach that stretched for more than a mile. On large rocks a few yards from the shore, children played. And people walked along the beach. About a quarter mile down the beach, on the right, were various shops. The village had been set down in what appeared to be a hollowed out mountain. Facing the ocean, houses jutted out of the sides of the mountain. Music blared out from the various shops along the beach and the village looked picturesque.

During the daytime, lectures included information about African culture including the Muslim way of life. I met with the others for lectures in one of the few structures with a roof. The ceiling was one of the first things I noticed. Inside was a long wooden conference table and chairs, an easel, floor to ceiling length windows that opened out on a view of the ocean, and bottled water sitting on a side bar.

I took water and a seat at the head of the table close to where the lecturer stood, and discovered the entire ceiling covered with small white and brown sea shells; no space was left uncovered, and I thought this to be the most intricately set wall design I had seen. It was fascinating.

On one occasion, the lecturer was a young thin man with wire rimmed glasses and a dark complexion. He discussed the emergence and spread of Islam throughout Africa which predated Christianity. Another time the lecturer was female; she was petite with soft eyes, light brown skin, natural hair that she pulled back into a large Afro puff, and lively hands used to make dramatic points. She discussed Muslim religious beliefs including polygamy. She said, "All women do not go along with polygamy, but women in general are aware this is permitted.'"

The impactful views and cultural scenes in Senegal had revived in me a textual pleasure similar to that gained from reading a good book, but the magnificent dance on the final night seemed to help put it all into perspective.

It began in the village clearing where the group had first arrived. Upon our arrival, there was nothing noteworthy about it since I had not paid attention to or noticed the round structure's presence; in fact, the small arena-like structure was obscured by dark curtains that covered its outside and it could very well have been mistaken for a large storage area. In the afternoon sun on this day, the structure became more visible as folks dressed in tights, ventured in and out of its side door. Using limited English and curving their arms toward the open door, the dancers beckoned the group to come inside.

Inside looked like a small stadium: a circular dance floor graced the middle of rows of benches that curved around and upward; lights were affixed at the top. Thick dark curtains curved around the back of the entire roofless structure. Several very darkly pigmented young men drummed while several young, dark-skinned, very thin dancers practiced dance moves in the middle.

The drummers smiled as several group members moved toward them. They began a slow beat of island sounds that seemed to motivate body movement. I was directed by a young skinny man, later identified as the instructor, to move the lower half of my body as dictated by the music. He raised his hands, rocked his hips, and motioned with a slight head nod. With a quick dance, he led the group, that ventured slowly toward him. Picking up his signal, we began a slow hip sway.

For an hour, we practiced rhythmic body movements, as the instructor and the drum beats cajoiled us; and then we went to lunch. On this beautiful sunny day, the abundance of trees in the village coupled with the breeze off the ocean created a cool atmosphere inside and out despite the ninety-degree temperature.

After dinner, Niama and I heard the drum call to come to the clearing. Once there, we were ushered inside the brightly lit stadium. Niama lifted her chin toward the seats on the upper level. I said, "I guess we can see everything from up there."

Folks from all over the village appeared, trickling toward those gathered inside. The seats began to fill quickly as the evening light faded into darkness.

To the beat of drums, under the lights, young male and female dances, slim with limber chocolate brown legs, began slow movements. They lifted their legs outstanding heights similar to break-dance and moonwalk routines.

A professor joined in while the audience began to shout; the drumming got harder and as the dancers encircled the professor, he began an oscillating hip thrusting motion that seemed to signal others forward. More audience members joined the circle of dancers to move with them and around them, close to them and beside them. The shouts became a crescendo. The dancing filled the night; the drumming was spectacular and so were the artistic movements of the dancers. Young and old people, more than I had imagined, were in the village. But the dancing was the focal point and it captured me, as well as, it seemed, the others. The dance movements called the audience, and the audience responded back. Most of those present moved. From the reaction of the crowd, the dance was a spectacular affair.

Well after 10:00 PM, the group returned to our bungalows.

Niama said, "How you feeling?"

"Good. The energy from the dance makes it easy to pack." As I climbed the stairs to the bungalow ahead of her, I looked back and smiled.

"Oh yeah," she said.

In the clearing the next morning, where we had first gathered under a calm blue sky, the village natives sold their wares of leather wallets, straw bags and jewelry. The bus arrived, and as we boarded and made our way up and around the winding path to the main road, I felt good about our adventure. *The movement of the dancers had to come from innate ability—something so smooth and spectacular that it could be passed on and on.*

I strongly believed that dance transmitted to urban youth in the US through epic memory—long memory that had remained intact, inside those young people whose ancestry had hailed from Africa. Especially when I considered Battle Dancing, the moves of Michael Jackson, and the youth imitating him at block parties. *That ability had survived the middle passage, and it would remain shut up in the bones of the people who looked like me.*

That was culture, and I would take that with me to infuse into mentoring opportunities. The second time around in Africa made me dance. Dancing made Africa most memorable. Like *Sankofa*, dancing must be practiced. Lest we forget.

ABOUT THE AUTHOR

Marlene Archie was raised in Philadelphia, Pennyslvania and has taught at several universities including Cheyney, Drexel, Temple, and Arcadia. She earned a Ph.D. in African American Studies at Temple with the desire to touch young minds inspiring them to "know thy self." To edify human values through literature that invokes, arouses, and celebrates the global African American presence is her heart's desire. She has authored numerous articles on the African American experience, founded Charter Schools that embrace the culture, and remains a community activist-scholar in her hometown where she resides. She is the mother of two sons.

www.ingramcontent.com/pod-product-compliance
Lightning Source LLC
Chambersburg PA
CBHW050455110726
47899CB00003B/956